THE COWBOY IN UNIT E

Mockingbird Place

LEE SWIFT

Acknowledgments

This is dedicated to my mother. She's my hero, my mentor, my advisor, my motivator, and my best cheerleader.

I love you, Mom!

Mockingbird Place

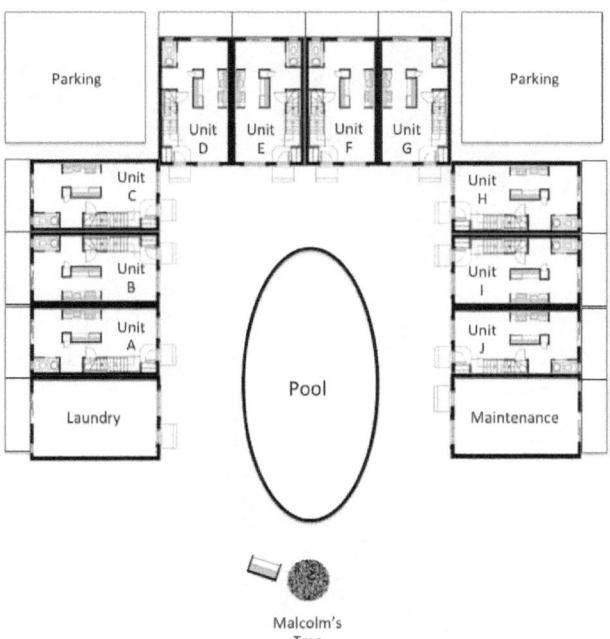

Malcolm's
Tree

I stand by my front window, where the light is best this time of day, gazing at the white void, praying for inspiration. The blank canvas taunts me. Where to begin? It's always like this when I start a new painting. It has to mean something. I need feeling and life. Right now, all I have is emptiness.

My roommate and best friend, Jackson, always teases me about my process—or in his words my "idiosyncrasies." My last painting took me over a month to complete, but the first ten days was like this one, staring at the canvas before I pressed a brush filled with paint to its surface.

Out of the corner of my eye, through the window, I see one of my new neighbors walking up the sidewalk. Ava Stone is pregnant and is carrying a big box. In her current condition I wonder if she should be lifting heavy things.

She and her good-looking cowboy, Luke Wagner, are moving into the apartment next to Jackson's and mine—Unit E. That leaves Oliver's old apartment, Unit F, as the only vacancy at Mockingbird Place. I met the couple at the complex's yard sale when they were taking a look at the apartment. They were living in a motel so that Ava could start her classes at the university on time until they could find a place to rent. Ava and Luke's new home had been empty for quite some time. Until now. I'm glad it's finally going to be occupied and hope the new couple will be good neighbors. And most of all I have to stop thinking about one of them.

I've never been attracted to cowboys before, but there is something about Luke that I can't quite seem to shake. But I need to. He's obviously taken and straight.

When Ava smiles at me as she turns to go into her apartment, I wave.

Glancing back at my canvas, I feel so frustrated. I'm no closer to an idea than before. Why do I do this to myself? No one will ever see this work when it's completed. This painting is for my eyes only now that Malcolm is gone. He was the only one I was ever comfortable sharing my work with. He got it. He knew what I was trying to say with each piece.

Like everyone else at Mockingbird Place, I thought he would live forever, even though he was eighty-two when he died. In June, we had his memorial in the courtyard and planted a tree in his honor near the pool.

I see Ava heading back to the parking lot and wonder how many more boxes she and her boyfriend have to unload. I decide to finish my coffee before I put my brushes away and help them.

I step back from the blank canvas. Should I paint another portrait of Malcolm? No. I just can't bring myself to paint him again. It hurts too much. I need more time. Right now, I could use an idea for this canvas, but I'm at a total loss. Damn it.

My art continues to be therapeutic for me. When I was twelve years old my counselor suggested art therapy and I found my passion. I can place myself inside my paintings, feeling the breeze on my skin or hearing the crashing of the waves on the shore. I'm there and I don't feel the pain. Still, my paintings allow me to gaze into the darkness of my past. They also help me release the tension and anxiety.

Actually, I wish all of my paintings could remain private. Each is so personal and carries its own meaning. Whenever anyone looks at my paintings I feel exposed and vulnerable. *Dirty.* I wonder if people can see my younger self weeping from the despair in my brush strokes. I definitely can, no matter the composition I've created, whether beach or mountain scene, whether wild animal or newborn baby, whether impressionistic or realistic. Each painting carries drops of the pain from my past.

Two of my pieces were on display for my professors to judge. I wonder if it was worth the As I got on both, because it nearly wrecked me until I was able to take them back to my storage unit. That's where I keep my completed paintings.

This semester is so much better than last. I have a fantastic schedule and only have to be on campus two days a week. The rest of the week is mine. All mine. And the classes that I am taking don't require students to create and present a work of art, unlike last semester.

As I put my empty cup down, I see Ava collapse and the box she was carrying crash to the ground.

A blast of electricity shoots through my body, and I toss my brushes aside and rush out my door.

"Ava. Ava." I lift her head off the ground and start shouting for her boyfriend. "Luke. Get out here. Ava has passed out." *Where the hell is he?*

Her eyes open. "What happened?"

"You passed out and fell," I tell her.

"Oh no." Ava rubs her hands over her belly. "Thank God, I just felt a kick. I think the baby is fine."

Kick or not, I know she needs to see a doctor. "Where's Luke?"

Before she can answer, I see him running up the sidewalk.

He kneels down next to me and shoves a sack in my chest. "My God, Ava, what happened?" he asks in his thick West Texas accent. "Are you okay?"

"I'm fine. I'm fine. Everything is fine." It's very clear how anxious she is despite her words. She probably doesn't want her boyfriend to worry.

"I'm not so sure about that," I say. "She passed out."

She shakes her head. "You didn't have to tell on me, Mr....?"

"Trace Cotton, your next door neighbor, but please call me

3

Trace." I set the sack to the side and Luke and I help her up into a sitting position.

"Thanks for your help, Trace, but I need to get her to the hospital." Luke is clearly in a protective, possessive state of mind. I can't blame him. This cowboy seems to be one of the good guys.

Ava nods anxiously. "Yes. I want to make sure my baby boy is okay."

"Let me take you." I tell them, picking up the warm sack, which I notice is from Aunt Lucy's Diner. "I know the quickest route to the hospital."

Luke turns to me, his brown eyes filled with concern. "Perfect. You drive and I'll take care of her." He lifts Ava into his arms.

"I can walk, Luke," she says.

"Not until we get the doctor's okay."

I lead them to my car. Luke gets in the back with Ava. I sit behind the wheel, realizing I'm still holding onto the warm sack obviously containing what is meant to be their lunch. The aroma lets me know it is burgers. I place the sack in the passenger seat and start the engine. I drive to the hospital as fast as I can.

When we get to the hospital, I let them out in front of the emergency room doors. Despite her objections, Luke carries Ava inside.

I park the car and send a text to Jackson, who is still studying at the library, about what is going on. I walk into the waiting room just as a nurse is leading Ava and Luke through a set of double doors.

Anticipating that it might be a while before they come back out, I take a seat. Even though I only barely know Ava and Luke, they seem like a perfect couple. I hope Ava and their baby are okay.

My phone buzzes.

It's a text from Jackson. *Just left the library. Any word yet about our new neighbor?*

I type back an answer. *Luke just carried Ava into the ER. I'll let you know when we get word from the doctor.*

Do you need me to come to the hospital?

I can always count on Jackson. *I've got this covered for now. If something changes I'll call you. Otherwise, I'll see you at home.*

If you need me for any reason, let me know.

As I put my phone away, my stomach growls. I forgot to eat. Realizing Luke's meal will go bad, I decide to go back to my car and get their sack of burgers. After we finish here, I'll buy him and Ava fresh burgers.

I step to the nurses' station.

"May I help you?" the woman behind the desk asks.

"I came in with the couple who just went to the back—the cowboy and pregnant lady. I need to run to my car to get something. If they come out, would you let them know I'll be right back?"

"Of course, but you have plenty of time I'm sure."

"Thank you."

As I walk to the car my cell buzzes again. This time it's a phone call—from Martha.

"Hey, Martha." I open my door and grab the sack.

"I just got a text from Jackson about Ava," Martha says in a tone full of concern. "S found the box on the sidewalk Ava dropped when she passed out. Do you know how she's doing?"

"No word yet but we haven't been here very long." I'm not surprised Jackson sent her a text. One thing about Mockingbird Place you can always count on is—*we take care of each other*. Sometimes that can appear like we are into each other's business too much, but whatever is done comes out of love, especially with Sarah and Martha, who we all lovingly call S & M. "What can S and I do to help?"

I walk back into the waiting room and sit in the same chair. "We left so fast I know I didn't lock my door and they didn't lock theirs either."

"S and I already took their box back inside Unit E and locked their door. I'll lock your door when we get off the phone. You don't worry about a thing here. Just take care of our new friends, Trace."

"I'll do my best."

After we say good-bye my stomach growls again, this time more demanding than before. As I walk to the soda machine to buy a Coke, I am reminded how lucky I am to be a part of Mockingbird Place's family. The 10-unit 1950s Mediterranean complex is not just where we live. It's our home. Most of the residents are gay and lesbian college students like Jackson and me. S & M are two of three owners of the complex and take care of everything and everyone. They are the center of our little family.

Oliver is the other owner, though he leaves the management to S & M since he's still in college. I'm so happy for him. He and Adam, our resident former-Marine, fell in love and are living in Unit A. We're all excited about their wedding. They're tying the knot this Saturday by the pool. It will be the second wedding there. The first was back in July for S & M.

Back in my seat, I pull out one of the two cheeseburgers but leave the fries. There's no saving them. They're cold and limp. After I finish the burger, I look at the time on my phone. Luke and Ava have been back there for at least an hour.

God, I hope she and the baby are okay.

Wanting to talk to someone to calm my nerves, I bring out my phone and see Malcolm's name at the top of my favorites list. God, I miss him.

I met Malcolm when I was eighteen and he was seventy-nine. It was at a student-parent mixer for incoming LGBT freshmen sponsored by the Rainbow Student Alliance. I didn't want to go. I thought it was going to be boring. But my counselor and my parents finally convinced me I should attend. Their hope was that I might meet some other students who would make my transition to college easier. They were right, but it wasn't the students that made me feel more comfortable. It was Malcolm.

He'd come to the mixer as Oliver's guardian. My parents hit it off with him right away. When the three of them started talking, Oliver introduced me to some of his friends. We all agreed the party *was* boring. That's the night I learned Oliver intended to become the Rainbow Student Alliance's president one day.

"I know the parents and professors mean well, but I promise there will never be a dull party like this one ever again once I'm president." Oliver was elected president last year and is serving a second term this year. And he has lived up to his promise. The Alliance's mixers and parties and parades are so much fun and the membership has doubled since he came to office. After three gunmen attacked some of our members this summer, I was worried that the Alliance would fall apart and disband. But because of Oliver's leadership no one has left and more students are joining than ever before.

As the student-parent mixer started winding down, I found a quiet corner and began drawing a single rose complete with petals, leaves, and thorns on a napkin. Lost in my work, I was unaware that Malcolm had slipped behind me and was watching me draw.

When I finished, he said, "Very nice."

I immediately covered the napkin with my hand. "I was just messing around."

"You should mess around more. You've got real talent." He smiled. "I've always loved roses, especially red ones. But their thorns remind me not to take their beauty for granted. Very much like life, don't you think, Trace?"

"I do." I was stunned. Malcolm had put into words the feelings I had drawing the rose.

Malcolm understood what my paintings mean to me and most importantly, he understood me. He saw every single one I ever painted. But now he's gone and there's no one I can share them with anymore. I did a portrait of him last year. I could tell he wanted to keep it and hang it on his wall but he respected my privacy. Why didn't I go ahead and give it to him? No one had to know I was the one who painted it. I miss him so much. I could so use his advice right now.

Another glance at the time tells me it's been another thirty minutes since Luke took Ava through the double doors.

When I see Luke come out from the back smiling and holding both his thumbs up, I'm relieved.

He walks over to me and sits down. "Ava and the baby are fine."

"I'm so glad."

He places his hand on top of mine. That seems unusual to me, especially for a cowboy whose pregnant girlfriend is expecting their first baby. But maybe it's because he's so happy she's okay.

I leave my hand under his, wishing he were gay. "Honestly, I was getting worried because you were back there so long."

"That's because they were doing an ultrasound as well as checking her." His eyes light up. "You should see the baby. Little Mick is not going to be little. He's going to be a big boy."

"If he's anything like you, he will be. You've got to be at least six foot."

"Six-one, just like my brother. Everyone is pretty tall in my family." He leans back and removes his hand from mine.

I instantly miss his touch. Am I crazy? He's not available or even gay. Maybe he is just the touchy-feely type.

"Trace, you and I are about the same height, aren't we?"

"I'm six foot."

Luke picks up the sack from the table.

"I ate one of your burgers. I want to buy you and Ava fresh ones or I can pay you back."

"There's no way you'll pay us back, Trace. I'm so grateful you brought us to the hospital. I don't know what I would have done without you. I'm especially thankful you were there when she first passed out."

"Did the doctor say why she passed out?"

"Ava was so busy getting us settled into the apartment she forgot breakfast. That's why I hurried to get her lunch. Thank God, Aunt Lucy's Diner was so close to Mockingbird Place so I got back quickly."

"That reminds me." I pull out my phone. "I need to let Jackson and Martha know that Ava and the baby are fine."

As I fire off the text, Luke asks, "Jackson is your boyfriend, right? The guy you live with?"

"Nope. We're just roommates and very good friends."

"Mm. I thought you were gay."

I laugh. "I am gay and proud of it."

Luke nods. "I know that's right."

"I'm really not trying to be an asshole about it, but I *am* proud of who I am."

"You're absolutely right. We should be proud of who we are, Trace."

"Thanks for your understanding."

A nurse comes out from the back with Ava in a wheelchair.

Ava points at us. "There are my two knights in shining armor."

We stand and walk over to her and the nurse.

"Can you bring your car around?" the nurse asks.

"Certainly. I'll be right back." As I walk to my car, I glance at the hand that Luke touched. Why can't I find a gay guy like him? Good-looking and so kind.

Chapter 2

The warm water feels good on my skin.

As I finish my shower, my mind brings up an image of Luke again. God, I have to stop thinking about him. He's unavailable. He's with Ava. I'm so glad she and the baby are okay. She's a wonderful person. I really think if I can get a handle on my fascination for Luke that we could all be friends. Good friends.

I close my eyes and will the image of the sexy cowboy out of my head. I can do this. I must do this.

I get out of the shower and wrap a towel around my waist. The delicious aroma of coffee rises from downstairs, calling to me.

Once in the kitchen, I find Jackson at the sink, rinsing dirty dishes and placing them in the dishwasher. I sneak up behind him, knowing he hasn't heard me, and growl, poking him in the sides.

"Fuck!" He jumps and twists around, dropping his cup. It shatters when it hits the floor. "Trace, damn it." He punches me in the shoulder. "That cup was my great-grandmother's. The last thing I have of hers."

"Oh no. I'm so sorry."

"Gotcha." He punches me again.

I smile. "You asshole."

He grabs a broom and dustpan. "I'm the asshole?"

"Let me do that." I hold out my hands. "I'm the one who scared you."

"I've got it," he says, which doesn't surprise me.

Jackson is a bit OCD. I'm not. Quite the opposite actually. That's why our friends refer to us as Oscar and Felix. It's not that I'm bad about keeping things picked up and clean. Hell, I even make my bed most days. It's just that Jackson has *his* way of doing things and doesn't know the words "moderation" or "compromise." The biggest fight we ever had was when I put away the groceries and didn't place the soup cans on the shelf with their labels facing out—in alphabetical order. Very dumb on both our parts. But our fights are usually about silly things, not that we have many. The longer we live together the less we have. I figure by the time we're thirty, we won't have any fights.

"Just pour yourself a cup of coffee and refill mine." Jackson dumps the shards from the broken cup in the trashcan. "I've got a few minutes before I need to leave for class."

I bring our coffee to the table, sit down, and take a sip from my cup. Then like every morning, I say, "Perfect. You make the best coffee."

He responds with his usual answer. "It's all in the beans. You have to grind them just before you make a pot and not any sooner."

We've been living together for two years. He's my best friend. I like what we have.

Jackson returns the broom and dustpan to their appropriate places, washes his hands, and joins me at the table. "I wish I had your schedule this semester. It must be great having classes only two days a week."

"It's really great, but Tuesday and Thursday are long days." Another sip and I start to feel human. "Did you and Ava decide to ride together?"

"We sure did. It will be nice to have her company on the way to class." Jackson offered to take her after the passing out incident, which was only yesterday. He's a very caring guy. "She told me that

Luke is still looking for work. Riding with me leaves their car free for him, so it's good for all of us."

Though Jackson and Ava don't have the same classes, their schedules are identical. Both start at nine and end at one.

"I was thinking we should ask them over. Maybe for pizza and beers. That way we can get to know them better."

Jackson grins. "Ava can't drink, Trace."

"Right. We can have tea or soda for her. I'd like to know what they enjoy doing. Maybe they're movie buffs like you and me."

"Or maybe I could teach them how to play Pitch."

I groan. "Please, not that silly card game your family likes to play."

"You're only groaning because you don't know a queen from an ace."

I smile. "Very funny."

Jackson has tried to get me to play with him ever since we met. *My junior high coach liked card games. Asshole.* That's the reason I don't like playing cards.

"Great idea. I'll talk to her about it on the way to campus this morning. How about tonight?"

"I'm free. The only thing on my list is to see if I get inspired to put some paint on that damn canvas by the window."

"You always do this when you start a new piece. You get worked up until you drive yourself crazy. Why don't you just relax? I'm sure it will be fantastic."

"I hope you're right."

He smiles. "I'm always right. You should know that by now, Trace."

I laugh. "I know that you *think* you're always right."

Our doorbell rings.

"That's Ava." Jackson grabs his backpack and walks to the door.

I think about going upstairs to grab a robe, but don't. I'm really enjoying this coffee and easing into the day. Jackson and Ava need to hurry if they are going to make it to class on time, so I know he's not going to invite her in. But if she does get a quick peek at me, I still have the towel wrapped around my waist.

13

Jackson opens the door and I see Ava and Luke standing on our steps. Luke is wearing shorts and nothing else. OMG! He's so hot. Tan. Muscular. Wow. *And Ava is having his baby.*

"Hey, Jackson." Ava sticks her head through the door and looks me in the eyes. "Hi, Trace. I brought Luke over. He thinks there's a water leak in the wall between our units."

"A water leak?" Jackson shakes his head. "I better get S & M to open up the maintenance room so I can get a key to turn the water off to the building. Come on in."

Ava and Luke walk in.

I stand, making sure my towel is secure. "I got it. You and Ava go to class. I'll take care of this."

"We've already proven that you and I are good in a crisis, Trace." Luke winks at me. "I'll help you."

Damn, why does he do this to me? I need to get a handle on my feelings for him. That's a dead end I don't need to walk down. I'm not the kind of guy who breaks up couples. And besides, Luke isn't even gay. *So get a grip, Trace.*

I turn to Jackson. "Go."

He and Ava leave.

When the door shuts, I turn back to Luke. "Where did you hear the leak?"

"In the wall," he says in that accent of his that drives me wild. "I was in the shower upstairs and when I turned off the faucets I could still hear water dripping. I pulled on a pair of shorts and came right over with Ava to see if you guys could hear it too in your apartment."

"That might have been me. The walls at Mockingbird Place are thin. I took a shower a while ago, too. That's probably what you heard."

"I bet you're right." He grins. "Just imagine, Trace. You and I were standing naked in our respective showers with only a thin wall between us."

I try to keep my cool but feel a wave of heat roll over me. *What the hell is it with this guy?* Ava leaves for school and he starts flirting with me. Screw that. I'm not into breaking them up even if Luke likes to play around. "I'll go upstairs to the bathroom and see if I can hear anything."

"I'll go with you."

"No," I say in a tone that comes out harsher than I intend. Softening my voice, I add, "Pour yourself a cup of coffee, Luke. I'll be right back."

I rush up the stairs, trying to get control of my desires. I know what the right thing to do is—ignore Luke's blatant come on. Ava is a sweet girl. I like her. I won't betray her, no matter how attracted I am to Luke.

Before listening at the bathroom wall for the possible leak, I drop my towel and get dressed. With clothes on I'll be better prepared to resist temptation.

I press my ear to the bathroom wall and hear water dripping. "Damn. There is a leak. Sounds like it's somewhere between the sink and the commode."

When I get back downstairs, Luke is staring at my blank canvas with a cup of coffee in his hand. The soft morning light illuminates his gorgeous body perfectly. God, he is perfect.

He turns my direction and our eyes lock. He smiles. "Jackson told Ava you were an artist. About to start a new painting I see. What is it going to be?"

"I don't know yet."

"I'd like to see it when you finish."

I can't let him see it. I can't let anyone see it. So instead of answering him, I say, "I heard your leak."

"*My* leak?" He laughs. "It's between our walls, Trace. That makes it *our* leak."

I can't help but grin. He's got a great sense of humor. "I suppose so. We need to call S & M." I pull out my cell. "The water has to get turned off to the building until Harvey can figure out how to fix it."

"Harvey?"

"Our maintenance man. Great guy." I hear Martha answer my call. I tell her about the situation. "Is Harvey on property?" I ask her, knowing he doesn't live at Mockingbird Place.

"Harvey's here with me and Sarah. I'll send him right over, Trace."

Harvey has a beautiful home in Highland Park. He and his late wife built it in 1950. He's hosted several parties there for us. Everyone knows he's only working here because he and Malcolm were good friends. It's really strange to me how Harvey has acted since Malcolm's death. He didn't come to any of the memorial services and no one knows why.

Less than a minute later, Harvey is at my door.

"Hey, Trace." Harvey has on jeans and a work shirt. A ring of keys is attached to his belt. He's in his late 70s but you would never know it. He's got so much energy and can out last all of us in the stamina department.

"Hi, Harvey. This is Luke Wagner. Luke, this is Harvey Nichols."

They shake hands.

"Pleased to meet you, Mr. Nichols," Luke says.

"Same here, but everyone around here calls me Harvey. So tell me about this leak, fellas."

"Let me take you upstairs to listen." I lead him and Luke to the bathroom. "Luke heard it first."

Harvey places his ear to the wall. "Sounds like a leak." He turns to Luke. "Do you mind if I take a listen from your place? Maybe I can pinpoint it better from there."

"Sure. Come on. Both you and Trace. Three heads are better than one."

I'm not sure that's true, but I'm curious to get a look at Luke and Ava's apartment.

"Good point," Harvey says, smiling. "Lead the way, Luke."

We follow him into Unit E. It's laid out as a mirror image of Jackson and my apartment. I'm impressed how nicely Ava and Luke have decorated it—warm furnishings and great artwork. As we walk up the stairs to the bathroom, I glance at some of their family photos. The largest in the center catches my eye—an image of Ava and Luke—she in a wedding gown and he in a tuxedo— kissing each other. That clears up one of my questions. They *are* married, even though I've never seen Luke wearing a wedding band.

Once inside the bathroom, Harvey places his ear to the wall. "Big leak. I believe it's right here." He points to a place on the wall to the left of the sink. "You guys listen and let me know if you agree."

Luke goes first. "I agree. Sounds pretty bad. What do you think, Trace?"

As he steps back, I take his place next to the wall. "Louder on this side. Yep. This is the place for sure, Harvey."

"That's what I thought." He gets a pen out of his pocket and marks the spot. "Fill up your tubs and some pitchers with water. No telling how long I'll have to keep the water off before this gets fixed."

Luke frowns. "More than a day?"

Harvey nods. "There are four cutoffs to the building. Yours only takes out two units, yours and Trace's. The last time we had a leak it was between Malcolm's place and Unit B. The cutoff for that side of the building takes out Units A, B, and C. That took a week."

"A week?"

"Maybe." Harvey shrugs. "Maybe not if we're lucky. Old pipes. You open walls and end up discovering lots of other problems. We had to re-plumb both those units."

I can tell Luke isn't happy. Not one damn bit. I've already witnessed how protective he can be with Ava. Why can't he be that concerned with honoring his marriage vows to her?

"Harvey, Ava is pregnant." He shakes his head. "This isn't going to work. She's due next month. We just moved in. She needs a bathroom."

Harvey puts his hand on Luke's shoulder. "You won't have to worry about a thing. You'll see. You got about fifteen minutes before I cut the water off. I'll be back with some tools."

Harvey walks down the stairs and out the door, leaving me alone with Luke, who looks completely mystified.

"Harvey tells me not to worry. How am I supposed to do that? Ava needs water."

"I know what Harvey means, Luke. Everyone at Mockingbird Place sticks together, especially in a crisis, and a pregnant woman without a bathroom is a major crisis. We'll find a solution. Trust me."

Luke smiles. "I do trust you, Trace. I trust you very much." He pulls me in close and presses his lips to mine.

I push him back, anger mixed with desire rolling through me. "What the fuck are you doing? Get the hell away from me." I'm furious he has put me in this position.

"What? What's wrong? I guess I misread you. I thought you were as interested in me as I am in you."

"How can you even say that? You and Ava have a baby on the way. Grow up. You have a family who is depending on you, cowboy."

"But Trace—"

"I don't care what you have to say. Just leave me the hell alone." I bolt out of the bathroom, down the stairs, and out of his apartment—*his and Ava's apartment.*

Chapter 3

Gripping my paintbrushes, I glare at my blank canvas. But I'm not seeing the white surface. I'm seeing red. It's been hours since I left Luke after he kissed me and I'm still just as upset as when it happened. *Asshole.*

The water is still off. Harvey took down the sheetrock from Luke's side. I heard the racket but stayed on my side. I don't want to see Luke.

Jackson walks in and places his backpack on the counter. "I got your text. What's the verdict?"

"The verdict is Luke Wagner is a complete and utter asshole."

"I was asking about the water, but what happened between you and Luke to get you so pissed off? I've never seen you this way before."

"I don't feel like talking about it." I sigh. "You want to know about the water. Harvey came over about thirty minutes ago and gave me an update. The plumbing between our apartment and Unit E has to be replaced. Two days without water at least. Sarah and Martha are giving the four of us a key to Oliver's old place so that we can shower and get ready in the morning. I think I'll let Ava and her asshole cowboy use Unit E's bathroom. I'll ask Chad and Josh if I can use their bathroom until the water is back on. You do what you want."

Jackson places a hand on my shoulder and in a kind tone says, "What I want is for you to tell me what's going on with you and Luke. Talk to me, Trace. Don't shut down. I'm here for you."

He knows me better than anyone. It's hard for me when my emotions are so strong. I feel exposed.

"Come on, Trace. Let me in. Please."

I take a deep breath. "Fine. The asshole kissed me."

"What asshole? Luke?"

"Yes, Luke. Can you believe it? The minute Ava is out of sight he starts flirting with me." I recount everything that happened. "So you see why I'm livid."

Jackson's eyes widen and he smiles. "Oh no, Trace. You... thought that..." And then he starts laughing hysterically.

"What the hell is so funny?"

But Jackson just keeps on laughing, which only makes me madder.

"I don't screw around with married men, Jackson. I don't see what's so funny about that."

He finally gains his composure and sits down on our sofa. "Luke and Ava aren't married. They are just friends."

"Whatever. Friends with benefits. Jackson, she's having his baby. Luke is a total jerk."

"You don't get it. They're not a couple and they're not having sex. The baby isn't his."

"That's not possible. I saw their wedding photo. They were kissing."

Jackson's face darkens. "I'm sorry. I should have told you yesterday. Ava shared it with me when I asked her if she would ride with me to class."

"Shared what, Jackson?"

"She was married to Luke's twin brother. They were identical twins."

"You can't be serious." Realization of my mistake hits me like a ton of bricks.

"Very serious. Luke is gay just like you thought. In fact, he's big in the gay rodeo circuit."

My gut tightens. "I feel like a complete idiot. They *were* identical twins?"

"Yes. Ava told me about Mick dying in a car crash a month after she married him. A drunk driver hit Mick's car. The guy was also killed. She and Mick had already gotten their acceptance letters from the university. Ava didn't know she was pregnant until a few weeks after Mick's funeral. She and Luke were devastated. The three of them were so close. Ava and Luke clung to each other for support. Luke's the one who encouraged her to go ahead and start college. That's why he moved here with her, to give her the help she'll need with the baby and classes. He's put his rodeo career on hold, since it requires so much travel."

"God, what an amazing guy."

"He sure is. Ava is so grateful for all he's done for her."

I think about how I left things with Luke. "Shit. I can't believe I acted like such a jerk."

"It's an honest misunderstanding. You didn't know Luke had a twin brother."

"No, but I didn't give him a chance to explain either. I was so sure Luke was wanting to cheat on Ava that I left before he could say anything." I place my paintbrushes down and cover the blank canvas. "I've got to fix this…but how?"

"Just start by knocking on the door. It will come to you what to say."

"Maybe. If he'll even let me in. I was a real asshole."

Jackson smiles. "You like him, don't you?"

"Yes, I do. I've been fighting my attraction to him since the day they showed up at the yard sale to look at Unit E."

"This is good." He grins. "This is so good."

"What do you mean it's good? I just blew it with him."

"You don't know that until you go over there, Trace."

"You're right." I take a deep breath. "Wish me luck."

"You got it." He pats me on the back. "Remember, *he* kissed you. I think it's going to be fine."

"I hope so." I walk out and up to Unit E.

After I ring the doorbell, Ava opens the door. "Hi, Trace. Come on in. I'll get Luke for you."

It's clear she and Luke have already talked about what happened.

"He hates me, doesn't he?"

She grins. "Hardly. It's an honest mistake. Luke and I just never thought how it looked to everyone when we moved in."

"Why would you? That should have been the last thing on your mind after losing Mick."

She nods and closes her eyes. It's obvious she's still struggling with her grief.

"You and Luke have been through so much."

"Yes, we have. He's been my rock. I don't know how I would have survived without him."

"And I bet he could say the same about you."

"I hope so. He and Mick were very close. Luke and I just take one day at a time. Friends have told me it gets easier. I don't know if that's true or not." She wipes a tear from her eye and glances down at her belly. "But this angel needs me to be strong." She looks at me. "It's going to be okay with you and Luke. Trust me."

"I sure want you to be right."

"Have a seat. I'll send him down to you."

She goes up the stairs and I move to the sofa.

I'm so upset with myself. How could I make such an idiotic mistake? I should have let Luke explain instead of running away. But of course I didn't. With my history, it's not surprising that I screwed up. I always expect the worst. I've had to. It's how I protect myself. But then along comes a great guy like Luke and I ruin everything. Hell, Jackson, my best friend in the world almost walked away because of me shutting him out. Damn these walls I've built around myself.

I look up and see Luke coming down the stairs alone. He's still wearing the shorts from this morning, but now he also has on a black T-shirt.

"Hi," he says as if nothing is wrong between us, though there's something different in his tone that makes me wonder. The warmth I've felt with him before is gone and in its place there's a cold distance.

"Luke, I'm so sorry. I had no idea about your twin brother." I stand.

He crosses his arms. "There's no need to apologize. It's completely understandable," he states flatly. "I should have told you."

"I didn't give you a chance to tell me."

He shrugs. "Don't worry about it. We're good."

I'm getting a dose of my own medicine. Luke is shutting down —shutting me out. "It doesn't seem like we're good to me."

"Sure we are. Don't worry about a thing. Go on home and I'll see you around." Luke walks to the door and opens it.

I step right in front of him, ready to go out the front door, but then decide it's time for drastic measures. I wrap my arms around him and move to kiss him, but he pushes me away.

Completely frustrated and confused, I step back. "Damn it, Luke. Why are you being this way? This morning you were sending signals that you were interested in me, but now you're acting like a complete ass. I'm sorry about how I left things earlier, but when I saw that picture of Ava and your brother's wedding I assumed... well, you know what I assumed. I'm really sorry but I've told you that already. What else do you want from me?"

"I don't want anything from you, Trace. I don't mean to be a jerk, it's just something you said before you left this morning woke me up."

"Something I said?"

"Yes. You reminded me of why I'm in Dallas in the first place. There's a baby on the way—*Mick and Ava's baby.* You told me to grow up. You were right. Ava and her baby boy are depending on me, Trace, and I intend to be there for them."

"Of course you will be, but I don't understand what that has to do with you and me."

"I like you. I really do. It's been very tough since Mick died. You were the first person that helped me smile again. I really want to be friends with you. You have to understand that, but it can't be any more than just friendship between us, Trace, because I intend to ask Ava to marry me."

Chapter 4

Walking out of Unit E and away from Luke, I can't wrap my head around what he told me. He can take care of Ava and the baby, but that doesn't mean he has to marry her. I love how noble he is, but self-sacrifice to that extreme doesn't make any sense. It's actually a recipe for disaster. He has his life too. Does he intend never to fall in love?

When I open the door to Jackson's and my apartment, I find him sitting on the sofa next to a guy I've never met before. Nice-looking man with thick hair, dark skin, and blue eyes—definitely Jackson's type. I normally don't mind when he brings someone home, but right now I need him. Alone. I need to talk to him about what Luke told me.

"Hey, Trace," Jackson says. "This is Brad Duncan. He's on the tennis team with me. He dropped in to talk about our new coach."

Guessing it was probably more than just discussing the new coach that brought Brad here, I shake his hand. The way Brad's looking at Jackson makes it very obvious the real reason he dropped in on him. Brad's got the hots for Jackson.

"Nice to meet you, Brad."

"Same here. Jackson told me you're an artist." He points to my canvas by the window, which is still covered and without a single drop of paint. "I'd love to see one of your paintings."

Jackson frowns.

"I don't share my paintings," I say flatly.

Jackson looks at Brad. "I already went over that with you. He doesn't show anyone his work. Not even me."

Brad shrugs. "It was worth a try."

"You're trouble," Jackson says, and then turns back to me. "Go grab a beer and join us."

"Thanks for the offer but I better pass." I'm not in any mood for small talk. I need time to myself.

"Okay, buddy. I get it. Plenty of beer in the refrigerator if you change your mind." Jackson can read me like an open book.

I go upstairs to my bedroom and shut the door. That jerk certainly isn't for Jackson. Jackson can do so much better than Brad. I pull the covers down, deciding to stretch out and take a nap. But once my head hits the pillow I know there's no way I'm going to be able to doze off. I can't get my mind to stop replaying Luke's last words to me.

"It can't be any more than just friendship between us, Trace, because I intend to ask Ava to marry me."

Luke has been through so much. Losing his twin, he's clearly not thinking straight. But what can I do about it? Not a damn thing.

I can hear Jackson and Brad laughing downstairs. God, I want Brad to leave so I can talk with Jackson. But from the sound of things, it doesn't seem like that is going to happen any time soon. Maybe I should go get a beer and bring it back to my room. Maybe several. But getting drunk has never worked to solve any of my problems before. I'm just left with a major hangover whenever I overindulge.

I stare at the ceiling. I need advice on how to handle this with Luke. Even if we end up just being friends, I don't want him to make the biggest mistake of his life. He deserves to find happiness.

I sit up. If Jackson isn't available, which he clearly isn't at the moment, I know two people I respect highly who might be. S & M care deeply about all of us, just like Malcolm always did.

I get out of my bed, pull the covers back in place, and fluff my pillows. My plan is to grab a six-pack, say bye to Jackson and Brad, and head over to S & M's place. But when I walk downstairs I find Jackson alone on the sofa.

"Where's your friend?" I ask.

"He had to take off. He's got a paper due tomorrow that he needs to finish."

"I'm glad he's gone, Jackson. He's an arrogant jerk." I take a seat next to him.

"He may be on the pushy side, but he's really a nice guy."

"So you say."

"Now who's being arrogant? What's the matter with you, Trace? Do you need my undivided attention?"

"I do want to talk to you but I know you deserve better than Brad."

"What do you know about anything?" Jackson's eyes narrow.

We rarely argue, but when we do the lid gets blown off. I don't want that to happen. I'm already a mess after talking with Luke.

"Jackson, I'm sorry. I don't know the guy. It's just after I left Luke I really wanted to talk to you. When I came in and saw him here, quite frankly, I was pissed. Dumb. I know, but it's how I felt."

"Don't worry about it." His tone softens and he stands. "Let's grab a couple of beers and you can tell me what happened."

"Definitely."

"And by the way, not that it's any of your business," Jackson says with a grin, walking to the refrigerator. "Brad is just a friend and he's straight. He's got a girlfriend. But I can tell that brain of yours is swirling. You saw how Brad looks and you thought right away that I was into him."

I smile back at him. "He could have been my twin. I remember how into me you were."

"Key word—*were*. I love you, man, but not that way." Jackson returns to the sofa with our beers and hands me one.

"Same here." We've always been better friends than boyfriends.

"Don't let your head swell up, but I think you're better looking than Brad."

"That's the nicest thing you've said to me in ages." I take a sip of my beer. "You may have trouble believing this, but Brad is really into you—girlfriend or not."

"Maybe. But let's talk about Luke. What happened?"

"He told me that he wants to marry Ava."

"You've got to be kidding."

"No. He feels obligated because of his brother." I sigh, feeling lost and not sure what to do next. "He accepted my apology, said he understood but that we could only be friends going forward. Nothing more. And to top it off it was something I said when I blew up at him that brought him to that conclusion."

"What in the hell did you say?"

"That he needed to grow up. That there was a baby on the way that needed him. That Ava needed him."

Jackson shakes his head. "Trace, you've dug yourself a very deep hole."

"Yes, and I don't know how to get out of it." I take another sip of beer, my mind dredging up a terrible memory from my past. It was another time when I didn't have an answer or an escape. I shove it back down into that dark place inside me, a place where I keep all my pain stored. "Maybe there isn't a way out of this mess."

"What the hell do you mean by that?"

I plaster a grin on my face to hide what I'm really feeling. "Luke just kissed me, Jackson. It's not that big of a deal. After all, I just met him. We can be friends."

"Here you go again. You start having feelings for a guy and you completely shut down." Jackson's words push my buttons. "Luke's confused. He lost his brother. Give him a chance."

"No. I can't. Luke and me are a lost cause."

"Damn. Same old Trace. Waving the white flag."

"Better now than later. You and I attract guys like Luke and Brad who aren't really available for whatever reason. Maybe it's best we stay single. Besides, what we have together is good. Best friends. If you and I end up stuck with each other, that wouldn't be that bad. I can see us as two old men taking over for S & M and running Mockingbird Place."

"Damn it, Trace." Jackson slams his beer down on the coffee table, spilling the contents on the wooden surface. He stands, giving no notice to the mess, which is very unusual.

"Hey, I didn't mean to piss you off."

"But you did. You've pictured a future with me that won't ever happen. I won't settle for anything less than love and neither should you. Yes, you're my best friend. I love you like a brother, but I'm not giving up on love even if you are. No, I haven't found the right guy yet, but I will. Someday. And when I do, you and I won't be living together. I'll be living with my new husband."

"I know you're right, even though I dread the day that happens. I'll be happy for you. I will. I don't want to ruin your chance at happiness just because I can't find love."

"Listen to me. Love might be staring you in the face right now. Open your eyes. Take a chance. I know what happened to you was horrible, but you can't let that dictate the rest of your life. You have to learn to trust again."

"Easier said than done."

"Maybe so, but it doesn't change the fact that it's true. I've seen you repeat this cycle again and again. A guy starts getting serious and you sabotage any chance of something more. You're attracted to Luke. I've never seen you act this way about anyone."

"Yes, I am attracted to him. He's perfect."

"Then don't mess it up this time. I don't know if Luke's the right guy for you or not, but you'll never know if you give up on him."

"But he wants to marry Ava. What can I do?"

Jackson places his hand on my shoulder. "You can let him know how you really feel about him. If you don't, Luke's going to make the worst mistake of his life."

"I'll think about it."

"Good." Jackson's eyes fix on the spilled beer. "I need to clean this up."

As he walks into the kitchen to get a cloth, I wonder if there's anything I can say to change Luke's mind.

NERVOUS AS I'VE ever been, I knock on Luke's door.

Ava opens it. She looks beautiful in her yellow maternity dress. "Hey, Trace."

"Is Luke around?"

She shakes her head. "He just left for the grocery store. The minute I said I had a craving for chocolate ice cream he jumped up and rushed out for the store. I have to be more careful about what I say around him. He doesn't want me to want for anything." She grins. "But I really did want that ice cream."

"Luke is such a good guy, Ava. He just wants to take care of you."

"I know, but I'm not helpless. I can take care of myself. Why don't you come in and wait for him?"

I consider it, but I don't want her to notice how nervous I am. Besides I need to talk to Luke in private. "I would but I have a paper I need to finish for class tomorrow. Would you just have him call me?"

"Of course."

LUKE NEVER CALLED.

Since I didn't sleep any last night, I pour a third cup of coffee for myself to keep me awake for class. "This is definitely going to be a very long day."

With his own cup of coffee, Jackson sits at the kitchen table. "I know you're upset because Luke didn't call, but I bet there's a good explanation. Why don't you ask Ava when she gets here?"

"Do you really think I should?" I sit down opposite him.

"Yes, I do."

A knock on the door lets us know she's arrived.

"She's early." Jackson heads to the door. "Now's your chance."

"Maybe Luke will be with her."

But when Jackson opens the door, I see she's alone.

"Hi, guys."

"Come in, Ava," Jackson says. "We have time for a cup of coffee before we leave."

"That sounds perfect. I haven't had my one cup the doctor allows me yet." She sits down next to me. "Did you finish your paper, Trace?"

I nod. "I am going to give it another quick read through before I head to class."

"You could ride with us if you'd like, Trace." Jackson hands Ava a cup of coffee. "That would give us a chance to talk on the way to school."

I know Jackson so well. He's trying to take charge and fix things and thinks the ride to campus would give me a chance to ask about Luke. But I need to take care of this myself. "I would but since my last class is at three, two hours after you and Ava get out, I better take my own car. Ava doesn't need to stick around for that long waiting on me."

"I wouldn't mind, Trace," she says. "Just because I'm pregnant doesn't mean I'm can't hang out."

"I know, but I'm sure you have better things to do. Besides, I might have to stay later to talk to my professor." Still wondering about Luke, I ask, "By the way, did you remember to tell Luke to call me last night?"

"Yes, I did. Didn't he call you?"

Damn it. He's avoiding me. "No, he didn't. Maybe I'll catch him tonight."

SITTING IN MY CLASS, I'm not hearing one word Professor Adams is saying because I can't stop thinking about Luke. Why in the hell didn't he call me? Why is he avoiding me? But I already know the answer. He knows I think it's a mistake for him to marry Ava. How can I get through to him if he won't talk to me?

I need to tell Luke how I feel about him. Jackson is convinced that will turn him around and keep him from making the biggest mistake of his life. I'm not so sure. I don't know if he feels the same way about me as I do him. Regardless of how he feels about me, I still need to try to keep him from asking Ava to marry him.

Should I tell her what he's planning? No. That wouldn't be right.

"Trace?" Professor Adams is standing in front of me. "Are you okay?"

I look around at the empty classroom and realize how lost in my thoughts I was. "Sorry, Professor. I've got a lot on my mind."

"That's okay." Professor Adams has one of those smiles that can fill a room. "If there's anything I can do to help just let me know."

"Thank you, but I have to deal with this myself." I grab my backpack. "You said you wanted to talk to me after class."

"I have a favor to ask you."

I like Professor Adams. "Sure. What is it?"

"Would you reconsider letting me share one of your paintings with a colleague of mine who owns an art gallery in Deep Ellum? Just one, Trace. I think if you dip your toe in the water you'll overcome whatever is holding you back. A lot of talented artists like you are insecure about showing their work. But believe me, you're the most talented student I've ever had."

"I'll think about it," I lie. "Thank you for believing in me."

Professor Adams means well, but he has no idea the real reason I can't show my work.

Chapter 5

Holding my towel and toiletry bag, I unlock the door to Oliver's old place with the key Martha gave Jackson and me. Luke and Ava have the other key.

After learning the truth about Luke, I've decided to take my showers at Unit F instead of at Chad and Josh's. I haven't stopped thinking about Jackson's suggestion about me talking to Luke. But I still don't have a clue what to say to him. I need to be extremely careful how I choose my words because I don't want him to make such a big mistake. He has good intentions, but marrying Ava is not the answer. I'm sure Luke loves Ava like a brother loves a sister, but that's not the kind of love you need for a marriage. Marriage should be between two people who are deeply and romantically in love with each other.

I walk into the apartment and glance around. Unit F is empty. It looks strange without Oliver's furniture. I wonder if it will ever look as good as it did. He's such a great decorator. But all Oliver's things are inside Unit A now, along with his good-looking Marine, Adam. Those two *are* deeply and romantically in love. Only a few more days left before they get married.

Jackson believes he will find love one day, and I agree. He's a great guy. He deserves that kind of happiness. God, will I ever be that happy with someone? Will I ever have the heart-racing, can't-think-of-anyone-else kind of love? I'm not sure. Maybe I'm not fit for love after what happened. Who would want a guy who can't fully trust anyone?

I walk up the stairs and make the turn to the second floor hallway, which puts me straight in front of the bathroom. I'm shocked to see the door wide open with Luke standing at the sink, shaving his gorgeous face in nothing but a towel.

He turns my direction. "Just finishing up, Trace." Luke's warm accent once again mesmerizes me. "I'll only be a couple of minutes."

"No rush. I'll sit down on the stairs and wait for you." I turn around and settle down on the top step, facing away from him. Looking at him one second longer is only going to make things more difficult for me. Luke is top-of-the-charts sexy *in clothes*. Out of clothes? He's completely off the charts.

I pull out my phone for a distraction, even though I don't want to call anyone or play any games. So I scan through my photos. But they aren't keeping my attention. Two memories, both of Luke, keep coming up in my mind. One is of him yesterday morning in nothing but a pair of shorts standing in my apartment drinking coffee. The other memory just happened. It's forever imprinted inside me like the previous one. Right now, he's behind me in nothing but a towel. It takes all my willpower not to go in there and rip that damn thing off of him.

Every sound he makes captures my full attention—the water running, his breathing, the razor scraping against his face.

The door shuts, which surprises me.

Confused, I turn around and stare at the light shining out from under the door. Luke obviously isn't shy about his body. Why did he shut the door? Is he struggling with his feelings for me as much as I am for him?

I think about going to my place and coming back later—*after he's gone*. Staying and waiting is driving me insane, and I still have no idea what to say to him. But before I get a chance to leave, Luke walks out of the bathroom in nothing but a pair of tight jeans that don't leave much to the imagination.

He sits down next to me on the step.

Silence.

"Trace, I—" Then he clears his throat.

"Do you have something you want to say to me?" I ask him.

"Yes. I just don't know how to." He looks down at his bare feet.

"Just let it out."

"Trace, I'm sorry that things turned out this way for us. I didn't handle it right. I've never been a very good communicator. That was my brother. Mick always knew just what to say in any situation. He was the life of the party. I always stood in the background. I'm usually better one on one."

"Like yesterday morning at my place."

"Yeah, but this time I'm having trouble." He looks at me with his big brown eyes. "I'm sorry about yesterday morning too. I know I came on strong. Usually I don't. Neither did Mick until he met Ava."

Sensing Luke needs to talk out his feelings, I ask, "How did they meet?"

He smiles. "She moved to our hometown when we were in tenth grade with her foster parents."

"Foster parents?"

He nods. "Ava's biological parents died when she was three. She grew up in many different households, but she never lost her zest for life. And every boy, straight or gay, in our high school was crazy about her. The straight ones wanted to date her, like Mick, and the gay ones, like me, wanted to be her BFF. Luckily, Mick and I each got what we wanted."

I'm so glad he's confiding in me about his past. "So how did your brother beat out the other boys?"

"He was so damn handsome. Just look at me." He laughs, which lightens our moods.

I grin. "You are handsome."

"So are you." He sighs. "Mick had spent all the money he'd made working with me the summer before at our neighbor's ranch.

He bought a 2009 Mustang. So he had to be creative to get Ava's attention. Every day he went to the florist and stole a rose petal to give her."

"Your brother sounds like a mix of a bad boy and a romantic."

"That was him with Ava for sure. Every day Mick sent her a rose petal with a note. Some of them he let me read. My favorite was the poem he wrote calling Ava his moon, stars, and everything."

"Damn. I couldn't resist that either."

"Neither could she, especially when he presented her a single red rose in our history class in front of everyone. They've been together ever since."

"And I know you and Ava are close."

"Very. She did become my BFF. Still is. In fact, I walked her down the aisle when they got married since she didn't have any family. I was also Mick's best man. It was the most beautiful wedding I had ever attended. The next month was the most wonderful time in Mick and Ava's lives. He confided to me that he'd never been happier, and Ava told me that she finally had the family she'd always dreamed of—a loving husband and a caring brother." Luke closes his eyes and his hands curl into fists. "Then the accident happened that turned our lives upside down. That drunk driver took Mick away from us forever."

I put my arm around Luke. "I'm so sorry."

"The very morning Mick was killed, he and Ava received their acceptance letters from the university. They were so excited about going to college, moving to Dallas, starting their lives. Two weeks later, Ava found out she was pregnant. She wanted to go to school to give the baby a better life, but she didn't know how to do it on her own. So I did what I needed to do—for her, for Mick, and for their baby. I quit my job on the ranch, let the IGRA know I wasn't going to rodeo for a while, packed up Ava and my things, and moved to Dallas. We both nearly lost it during the sonogram when we found out she was having a boy. She plans on naming him Mick."

"You're an amazing man, Luke Wagner. I can't even imagine that kind of pain. Thank God, you have each other. Ava needs you and you need her. But you don't have to get married to take care of her and the baby."

"But I do. The truth is the moment I saw you something ignited inside of me. You're a great guy, Trace. I wanted to get to know you better. I'd been under such a dark cloud since we lost Mick. All I wanted was sunshine and fun. And you were bringing that to me and I was getting lost in it. But then you reminded me of my responsibilities. My duty is to take care of her and the baby. My brother is gone. She has no one but me."

How can I get through to him what a mistake this is? "I totally get it. That is your responsibility, but like I said before you don't have to marry Ava to accomplish that, Luke. Can't you see that?"

"But I have to be completely focused on my duty to her and the baby."

"You still can be, just like you're doing now. You're supporting her so that she can go to school. You've given her a place to live. You're going to be there when the baby comes and will help her take care of it. I don't think she expects any more from you than what you are already doing."

"How can that be enough? She lost Mick. He was her whole world."

"But marrying her would stop both of your lives. Time would cease. You would be frozen in your shared grief for your brother. Neither of you could ever be with anyone you truly love. And though I'm sure she's not even thinking about finding someone new right now, she may in the future."

Luke stands. "You've made some interesting points, and I appreciate what you're trying to say. But you haven't been through this— losing Mick. Ava and I have. I will do what I have to do. I owe that to my brother's memory. In fact, I'm going to ask her tomorrow."

He hasn't asked her yet? Does Ava even know what Luke's plans are for her and him? "You can't be objective about this, Luke. Will you please at least see a counselor before you ask Ava?"

"I know you mean well, but my mind is made up." He leans down and wraps his arms around me.

I hug him back, unable to think of anything else to say that might help change his mind.

When he lets go of me and straightens up, our eyes meet. I can see in his face that this moment is good-bye.

And without another word, Luke walks down the stairs and doesn't look back.

Chapter 6

When Jackson and Ava walk out the door to drive to class, I strip my sheets off the bed and gather my dirty clothes. I'm in no mood to face the blank canvas right now. I just want to stay busy.

I didn't have a chance to tell Jackson what happened in Unit F with Luke last night. He was asleep when I got back. When I came downstairs this morning, Ava was already here.

Carrying my basket, I walk into Mockingbird Place's laundry room, a drab old space with gray walls and cement floors. There are three washers and three dryers, all white, a long silver table for folding, and four black chairs. This room is devoid of color. I keep promising my neighbors I'm going to paint the damn place to give it some color and life. The only solace to the space is the large window that lets in the sunlight.

This is the one job I always put off as long as I can. I hate doing laundry, unlike Jackson, who washes his clothes twice a week—six p.m. Monday and Thursday without fail. Still, I manage to get my laundry done before I run out of clothes. Today, I'm happy for the distraction. I hope doing laundry will keep my mind off of worrying about Luke and the mistake he's about to make.

All three dryers are running, but the three washing machines are empty. That means I can be done in an hour.

After placing my clothes in the machines and sitting down, I'm just as worried as I've been since Luke told me his plan. I rode with Jackson and Ava to the campus yesterday morning. I thought about asking her if Luke had popped the question, but it's none of my business. I didn't notice anything different about her demeanor, so I really don't think he has. Maybe he took what I said to heart and is considering seeing a counselor. I sure hope so.

Eli walks in with two empty baskets. "Hey, Trace."

"I was wondering whose clothes were in the dryers. Now I know."

He nods, opening one of them.

I've always liked Eli. He lives next to Jackson and me in Unit C. Eli is rarely home. Poor guy has the craziest schedule being a fireman. Eli is very laid back most of the time, but I have seen him lose it on two occasions. Both incidences happened when his ex came on the property. That guy is a total jerk. What Eli ever saw in him is a mystery to me and everyone else.

"How's that good-looking roommate of yours doing, Trace?" Eli's candid question shocks me.

"You mean Jackson?"

He smiles. "Of course I mean Jackson. You have other roommates I don't know about?"

"No. Just Jackson."

"Don't you think he's good-looking?"

"Sure, but I never think about him that way. He's definitely handsome though."

"Yes he is." Eli starts folding his clothes.

I smile, remembering the day Jackson and I moved into our apartment. Eli had definitely caught Jackson's eye. I wonder if the two of them might be right for each other.

S & M step into the laundry room with their clothes.

"Mine should be done in fifteen minutes," I tell them. "Then you can have all three washers."

"I'm pleased as punch about that." Martha places the basket she's carrying on the floor. "I absolutely hate doing laundry."

Knowing how much she likes her idioms, I reply, "We're on the same page, Martha."

She laughs.

"Eli, so glad to see you," Sarah says.

"I wish I could stay and enjoy this laundry party with you, but I'm due at the station at noon." He lifts his baskets of freshly folded clothes. "Don't have too much fun without me."

"We'll do our best," they say in unison and then kiss him on opposite cheeks.

When Eli walks out, I turn to them. "I'm glad you're here. I really need your advice on something."

"Anything you need, Trace," Sarah says. "M and I are always here for you kids."

"It's about Luke and Ava. You do know they aren't a couple, right?"

"Yes. When Luke filled out the paperwork to rent Unit E he told us about his twin brother."

Martha nods. "So sad what happened."

"When I first saw him I felt sparks and I believe he did too, but I thought they were a couple. So I ignored my feelings."

"But now you know." Sarah smiles. "I'm so happy for you. I think you and Luke would make a great match."

I shrug. "Maybe we would. But he's planning on asking Ava to marry him. He feels totally responsible for her and the baby."

"Doesn't he realize this is 2015?" Martha frowns. "She'll be just fine taking care of herself and the baby." Martha and Sarah's feelings about feminism are well known around the complex. They are two strong women who have survived so much. "Although I understand how he feels, Luke shouldn't try to take her independence away from her. Besides, he'll definitely be a part of Ava's and the baby's lives and we'll all be here to help out. In fact, S and I are planning a surprise baby shower for Ava."

Sarah takes Martha's hand and looks directly at me. "Trace, when did he tell you that he wanted to ask her to marry him?"

"The other night. We were in Unit F."

Sarah nods. "Ah. The water situation."

"Right. You should see him in a towel," I blurt out without thinking.

They both grin.

"I really like him," I confess. "And yes, I wouldn't mind going on a date with him. One of the many things I like about Luke is that he is such a good guy. It's wonderful that he's helping Ava so much. But even so, I don't want him to ruin his life despite all his good intentions."

One of the washers with my clothes starts buzzing and then the other two go off right after.

I start transferring my clothes to the dryers and notice S & M are whispering. I put my quarters in the dryers and hit the button. "The washers are all yours."

When Sarah's eyes meet mine, she says, "You just don't worry about a thing. M and I have an idea. We'll take care of everything."

"What kind of an idea?"

She and Martha grin.

"Just trust us," Martha says. "We've got this."

"Sure." I do trust them, but I still wonder what they're planning. They weren't there when Luke and I were sitting on the top of the stairs in Unit F. They didn't see the determination on his face.

As Martha places their clothes in the washers, Sarah puts her arm around my shoulders. "You really like him, don't you?"

"Yeah."

"That's good. Seriously, Trace, it's going to be okay."

"Not if he asks Ava today when she comes back from class."

"Good point. What time does she get back from school?"

"She and Jackson's last class ends at one. They usually get home by one thirty."

"Perfect." Sarah brings out her phone, clicks on a number I can't see, and then brings the cell to her ear. "It's ringing."

"Who are you calling, S?" Martha asks.

"Luke."

Martha nods. "This is going to be as easy as pie."

"Hi, Luke. This is Sarah. Would you be a dear and come to our place at eleven this morning? M and I want to throw a surprise baby shower for Ava and we want your input and help."

"Surprise baby shower?" I whisper to Martha.

"Yes. That was already in the works."

Sarah continues her conversation with Luke. "Plus, we'd love to make you lunch. It's the least we can do for you since you've been without water since Monday. So can we count on you?" She winks at us. "Wonderful."

I smile and say to Martha. "You two are devious."

"We are." Martha gives me a kiss on the cheek. "And we get results, Trace Cotton. Every time."

"By the way," Sarah says into the phone. "Harvey thinks he can have the water back on to your place and to Trace and Jackson's by tomorrow. Oh, he's there now? Good. That's great news. Okay. We'll see you at our place at eleven." She clicks off the call. "The water should be back on tonight."

"That is good news," I say.

"Harvey won't have the sheetrock and tile back up in Unit E's bathroom until tomorrow though."

"That's not a big problem, especially since the leak was between Luke and Ava's commode and sink. And at least we'll be able to shower in our own places." But a part of me wishes I still needed to shower at Unit F so I could bump into Luke again. "So how's this idea of yours supposed to work?"

"First, I'm going to go put some lunch together," Martha says.

"You?" Sarah smiles. "I'm the better cook."

"Says who?" Martha kisses her.

They've been together for decades but still act like newlyweds. Why not? They just got married.

"Okay, one of us will make lunch and the other one can finish the laundry."

"Honey, you can make lunch. I was just teasing."

"I know. Plus, I want Trace and Luke to have a slice of that delicious apple pie you made. And we still have some of that cinnamon ice cream to top it off."

My mouth starts to water. I've been lucky to enjoy S & M's meals many times. They are amazing cooks.

Martha gives me a hug. "This is so exciting. I love playing matchmaker."

"I thought we were just trying to get Luke to reconsider asking Ava to marry him."

"Yes. That too. But getting him to take a long, hard look at the wonderful man that lives next door—you—is also part of the plan." She kisses Sarah and walks out of the laundry room.

I laugh. "Your wife seems to have it all worked out in her mind how this is going to turn out."

"She always does. I need a cigarette. Care to step outside with me and get some fresh air?"

I'm not a smoker, but I love her company. "Of course."

There's not a cloud in the sky. A very light breeze rustles Malcolm's memorial tree.

She lights a cigarette.

"I hope you and Martha are right about this lunch with Luke. You didn't mention to him that I was going to also be at your place for lunch. I'm not sure how he will react to that."

"Don't worry, Trace. This isn't our first rodeo."

"I bet not. Did you know Luke set aside his rodeo career for Ava?"

She nods, taking a drag. "Quite the cowboy. He's done well in both the gay rodeo and pro rodeo circuits, winning several championship buckles. Did you know Luke rides broncos?"

"I didn't know that." An image of Luke in the arena on top of a bucking horse decked out in his cowboy clothes flashes in my mind. "Are you sure you and Martha can convince him not to marry Ava?"

"Trust me. M and I have conducted more than our fair share of what we like to call love ambushes. They never fail."

"Love ambushes? You two are devils."

She smiles. "Two of the best in Dallas, Texas."

We see Oliver and Adam holding hands, coming around the corner from the parking lot.

"And here comes two more of the best." She puts out her cigarette. "Hey guys."

"Hi," Oliver says.

Adam smiles. "Hey. How's it going?"

"Good," I answer. "Getting excited about the big day?"

"Yes, but there's still so much to do for the wedding." Oliver pulls out his phone and stares at the screen.

Adam smiles. "Not the list again, sweetheart."

"Yes, the list again, mister. Besides keeping up our grades in our classes, we've got to check with the florist, pick up our tuxedos, call the caterer, and get your mom and granddad at the airport. And that's just the rest of today." Oliver looks at Sarah. "I want to thank you and Martha for all your help."

She hugs him and Adam. "It's our pleasure. We're just happy for you both."

Oliver turns to me. "And you and Jackson have the chairs and tables covered?"

"We sure do. They'll be delivered Saturday at eight, and we'll make sure they're placed where you told us."

Everyone at Mockingbird Place is playing a role in the wedding, even Ava and Luke. She's in charge of making sure everyone signs the guest book and he's an usher.

Sarah looks at her phone. "Boys, it's about time for my clothes to be done and to put them in the dryers."

"Mine are probably done, too, and need to be folded."

"And we need to get going," Oliver says.

"I wish you would relax, honey. Everything is going to be fine." Adam kisses him lightly on the mouth.

As they walk into their apartment, I think about how much both of them have changed. Adam arrived at Mockingbird Place totally in the closet until spending time with Oliver. And Oliver was a serial dater until Adam moved into Unit A. They are so happy and so in love. God, I want what they have.

I quickly fold my clothes to have time to change and clean up before seeing Luke.

Sarah starts the dryers.

I lift my basket. "Bye, Sarah."

"I'll see you at eleven fifteen."

I walk out of the laundry room, hoping S & M's plan will work with Luke.

Chapter 7

I t takes me no time at all to put the clothes away, remake my bed, and pick out what I'm going to wear to S & M's lunch ambush. I grab a towel and my bathroom bag and walk over to Unit F. I just want to take a quick shower and freshen up before seeing Luke. I glance at his door as I pass by and once again an image of him atop a bucking bronco fills my mind.

As I start to unlock the door to Oliver's old place, Harvey walks out of Luke and Ava's apartment. Luke is with him.

Damn, this cowboy is sexy.

"Hi, Trace," Harvey says.

Luke turns my direction and smiles. "Hey."

A tingle rolls up and down my spine, a first for me. "Hi." I wonder if other guys get tingles like that.

"I was just telling Luke that I'll have the water back on in a couple of minutes," Harvey says. "If you can wait that long, you can shower at your own place."

"I can definitely wait that long." I put Unit F's key back in my pocket and walk over to them.

"Fellas, I'll be right back." Harvey hurries to the maintenance room.

"Boy, it's going to be nice taking a shower in my own bath-room," Luke says.

"Yes, it is." Should I tell him that I'm going to lunch too? I'm not sure him being ambushed is going to work out like S & M think it is. But if I tell him and he doesn't show up, all the work they did will be wasted. I can't let that happen.

"I hope Harvey hurries," Luke says. "I'm having lunch with S & M and I need a shower."

Now I don't have any choice. I have to tell him. "Me, too."

He smiles. "So they've recruited you for Ava's surprise baby shower?"

"I guess so. I'll be happy to help any way I can."

"That's just one of the things I love about Mockingbird Place. Everyone is ready to pitch in for each other."

"There's no place like it I've ever found."

Harvey walks back. "It's on, guys. Luke, I'll be back tomorrow to put the sheetrock and tile back up."

"Sounds great."

"Thanks, Harvey," I say.

Harvey leaves us once again.

"I'll see you at S & M's, Luke."

"You bet you will."

I watch him go inside his apartment, and then I walk into mine. Before heading upstairs to the bathroom, I call Sarah.

"Hello, Trace."

"Hi. Just wanted to tell you that Luke knows I'm coming to lunch. I ran into him and Harvey outside. Harvey turned the water back on to our apartments. Luke told me he was glad because he wanted to shower before having lunch with you."

"Ah. So you had to tell him. No worries, Trace. That sounds even better."

"What about yours and M's ambush?"

She laughs. "That's definitely still on. See you shortly."

I click off the phone and glance at the blank canvas. I finally know what I'm going to paint—the image of Luke on the bronco that won't stop playing in my mind.

I rush up the stairs to the bathroom and strip out of my clothes. But before I turn on the faucets in the shower, I hear the water start to run in Luke's bathroom.

Oh God. He's taking a shower too.

There's only a thin piece of sheetrock on my side that separates us. I wish I were Superman. I could sure use his X-ray vision right now to get a look at his gorgeous naked body.

I take a deep breath. I need to get a grip. He's going to ask Ava to marry him unless Sarah and Martha can convince him not to.

When I turn on the water, I hear him singing a Garth Brooks' song. I'm not really a country music fan but Luke's voice could change that. I step into the shower, enjoying the feel of the warm water on my skin, and Luke's singing gets louder. The tingle I felt earlier is back and has brought a bunch of friends. What am I getting myself in to? A cowboy with a country singing voice? That's never been my style—but *hello darlin'*.

Smiling, I start humming along with Luke as I wash my hair. Before I know it, I'm totally into it and start singing the chorus with him.

"Trace, you sound great." Luke's words come through loud and clear.

Damn. If I can hear him then he can hear me. "Um…thanks. I'm really not much of a singer, but you have an amazing voice."

"I think we're good enough to audition for *The Voice*."

I laugh. "I'm available next Tuesday."

I hear him chuckle. "I'm not sure we're ready for television. I can just see us on stage in the shower, naked, singing our hearts out."

Visualizing what he just said, I feel heat shoot down between my legs. "We better keep our duets to ourselves."

I hear him turn off the water on his side.

"I'll see you over at S & M's," he says.

"Okay." As I finish showering, I can't stop thinking about Luke. I really like him. Even us both taking a shower at the same time was fun and exciting.

After I dress, I look at the time on my phone. I need to hurry.

I knock on Unit I's door.

Sarah opens it and smiles. "Come inside, Trace. Luke and M are on the patio. She decided that the weather is so nice we should enjoy our lunch outside. Broccoli and cheese soup with a fresh salad and homemade rolls."

"That sounds delicious."

"What would you like to drink? We have beer, wine, tea, and sodas."

"Tea would be great."

We walk through the apartment, which is nicely decorated. One wall is filled with photos of Sarah and Martha over the years of their relationship. One of my favorites is the photo of a trip to Niagara Falls when they must have been in their twenties. Another is of them standing next to Malcolm under a disco ball wearing tight-fitting pants with flares. There are dozens of pictures, but my eyes fix on the newest addition to their display—a picture of S and M standing under Malcolm's memorial tree holding hands and saying their vows to one another.

Their choice in furniture is all about comfort. The two leather recliners sit side by side with a big flat screen television on the wall. At every party S & M have thrown for us, they insist on their guests sitting in their comfy La-Z-Boys. Along the opposite wall is a sofa in plush gold fabric with a large round brass table on a wooden frame they brought back from one of their trips to Asia. The entire space is warm and inviting.

Their unit is just like all the rest at Mockingbird Place with one exception. All of ours have a single door to our patios, but last year, Oliver and Malcolm surprised S & M with new French doors that lead out to their patio. Everyone likes them so well that Oliver has convinced S & M to put them in all the units. I can't wait until Jackson and I get ours.

I can see Luke and Martha through the glass doors. They're talking with big broad smiles on their faces. Have S & M already *fixed* things? Has Luke changed his mind about marrying Ava? Of course not. There hasn't been enough time. Just wishful thinking on my part.

Sarah hands me a glass of iced tea. "I can tell you're nervous about this, Trace. Just relax. M and I have been around the block many times. We know what to do."

"I know you do. I'm just anxious about how Luke's going to react."

"Trace, we're doing this out of a place of sincere concern for him. We care about him. You care about him. It's going to be fine."

Hoping she's right, I nod and we walk through the French doors to the patio. The table is all set with a red and white cloth over it.

My eyes lock with Luke's sexy browns.

"Hey, neighbor." He smiles.

"Hi." I extend my hand to him.

His eyes narrow. "Trace, we sang in the shower together. A handshake won't suffice."

He pulls me into a warm hug, and I wrap my arms around him.

"You sang in the shower together?" Martha is clearly surprised, and so is Sarah.

"Not exactly. Luke was on his side and I was on mine. We could hear each other through the wall."

"You should hear how well Trace and I sound together. Harvey is supposed to replace the sheetrock and tile, but I'm thinking we should leave the wall the way it is."

"I'm sure you do," Sarah says with a grin. "But the wall will be fixed. Ava definitely needs her privacy."

Martha motions for us to take our seats.

Luke pulls out a chair for Sarah. "This looks and smells delicious."

"It sure does," I tell him. "Both of them are amazing cooks."

"I just threw this together, boys." Martha sits down next to Sarah. "But wait until you get your teeth into my wife's wonderful apple pie. It's to die for."

Sarah hands the plate of homemade rolls to Luke. "And so are these. M's rolls are like crack. Once you have one you'll be hooked."

He laughs. "I'm sure I will be."

Martha ladles out the soup into our bowls. "Has Ava registered at any baby stores yet?"

He shakes his head. "Ava doesn't have any family. All she's done is made out a handwritten list of what we'll need for the baby."

"Can you get a copy of that list to us without her knowing?" Sarah fills our salad plates.

"Sure I can." He smiles. "You can't imagine how grateful I am that you want to throw a baby shower for Ava. She'll be thrilled. When are you planning on having it?"

"How about a week after Oliver and Adam's wedding? Right here at our place around noon. Will that work for you?"

"That will be great."

"I'm so excited about this. A baby boy at Mockingbird Place." Martha's eyes light up. "That angel will be spoiled rotten if S and I have anything to do with it."

Sarah kisses Martha on the cheek. It's very clear how thrilled they are about the baby. We all are.

She asks, "Do you know if Ava wants traditional blue or is she going for green or yellow?"

"Blue," Luke answers. "Definitely blue. It was Mick's favorite color."

I sense a sadness wash over him.

Martha reaches across the table and touches the back of Luke's hand. "I just want to compliment you on making sure Ava is able to get her education."

"I want to help her. She's my family."

"Well you certainly are helping her, Luke. With a degree, it's going to make being a single parent so much easier on Ava."

"Thank God this is 2015." Sarah puts her hand on Luke's shoulder. "She has so many more opportunities that M and I never had when we were Ava's age."

Martha nods. "A bright, pretty girl like Ava...there's no end to what she'll accomplish. Of course, we'll all be here for her and that precious baby boy."

"You don't have to worry about a thing, Uncle Luke." Sarah grins. "We're all family in this complex."

I realize that S & M aren't giving Luke a chance to respond. So this is how their *love ambush* works—keep talking and making your point and serving food. I'm too nervous to look directly at Luke to see how he's reacting to them, although I need to. I just don't want him thinking I'm a part of this ambush, even if I am in a small way.

"And some day I'm sure Ava's heart will heal, although she'll never forget your brother," Sarah says. "But she's a beautiful young woman and may fall in love again. But whatever her choices are, I'm glad she has the opportunity to pursue her dreams."

"Just listen to us go on and on." Martha winks at me. "What does a handsome cowboy like yourself dream about for your future?"

"I haven't thought about anything much except Ava and her baby," he answers flatly. "That's been my number one priority."

"And you've done such a fabulous job—moving to Dallas, getting the apartment, making sure she's in school." Sarah refills our glasses from the pitcher of tea. "But you've got to let Ava have her own space so she won't lose her independence."

Martha stands and gathers our dishes. "Don't forget, Luke, you need to start thinking about yourself and your own future."

His eyes narrow slightly. "I've already done that, Martha."

I realize that he's only fooling himself. He believes he has to sacrifice his future to take care of Ava and the baby. This ambush hasn't worked at all. He's still planning on marrying Ava. Damn. I need to come clean and say something to change his mind. But what?

"Does anyone want coffee with their pie?" Martha asks.

"Yes, please," he says.

I nod. "Me, too."

Sarah stands. "I'll handle the coffee, sweetheart. How about a scoop of cinnamon ice cream on your slices? M and I love it that way."

"Yes," Luke and I answer in unison.

They walk inside, leaving me alone with Luke.

I can tell he's thinking about what they said to him about Ava's independence. "Nice lunch, don't you think?"

"It was great. I appreciate them so much. You and everyone at Mockingbird Place have welcomed us with open arms. But the truth is I don't have time to think about myself. Mick is gone. Ava needs me. That's all that matters for now."

"For now? What does that mean?" Thoroughly confused, I ask him. "Are you still going to ask Ava to marry you?"

"Of course I am." He frowns. "I was planning on talking to a counselor like you suggested. But my mind is made up, Trace. I won't let Ava or Mick's child struggle. I will be there for them no matter what."

"But you don't have to, Luke. Can't you see that? Open your eyes. Look around. You're not alone."

"Is that what this lunch is really about? You told Sarah and Martha my plans and they're trying to get me to change my mind."

"No...well, maybe. But we do want to have a shower for Ava and the baby. We want you to know we're a family here. We'll help you and her in every way we can."

Sarah and Martha walk out with our dessert and coffee.

"Why the sober looks on your faces, guys?" Martha asks.

"I know what you are trying to do, and really appreciate it. But I still am going to ask Ava to marry me."

Chapter 8

I'm so upset how things turned out at S & M's lunch. The ambush didn't work. Luke is *still* going to ask Ava to marry him.

Filled with concern for Luke, I walk into my place with a slice of apple pie for Jackson that Sarah and Martha gave to me for him.

He is on the sofa with several of his textbooks spread out on the coffee table. "Hey, Trace. You okay? You look like you just buried your best friend, and that couldn't be it because I'm sitting right here."

I sigh. "I'm glad you're here, Jackson."

"Then out with it." He leans forward. "What's the matter? Did you get a chance to talk to Luke or not?"

"Yes, I did." I tell him about what happened in Unit F the other night.

"Damn, Trace. That's rough."

"Yes, it is rough. Very. And that's not all. I told S & M about his plans to marry Ava. So they had him and me over for lunch to talk about a surprise baby shower. On the flipside, they also subtly tried to show him that marrying her would be a big mistake."

"Subtly?"

"Yeah. Luke figured it out. He stayed for the dessert but left shortly afterward."

"Was he pissed?"

"No. He wasn't mad at them or me, but he was determined to follow through with his plan. Nothing we said could change his mind."

"Damn. That sucks."

"Yes, it does, but I think I know why Luke's doing this. He's not thinking clearly. He's still mourning the loss of his brother. And I have to admire his loyalty to Ava. I don't know anyone else who would sacrifice their entire life for another person."

"I have talked quite a bit with Ava since we've been riding to class together. She's never going to say yes to a proposal from Luke."

"How can you be so sure?"

"Because she's already made plans for her future, and damn good ones. She's strong. She's going to be fine."

A knock on the door startles us. I open it to find Ava, who appears to be upset.

"I need your advice, guys."

I put my arm around her. "Of course. We're here for you. Is this about Luke?"

She nods.

Jackson stands and rushes to us. "What's wrong, Ava? Where is he?"

"I don't know. He just left. He was so hurt." She closes her eyes and shakes her head. I can feel her trembling. "He asked me to marry him. What in the world was he thinking?"

It's very clear that Ava told Luke *no*.

"Come sit down with us." I wonder what Luke is feeling right now. He must be very confused.

We all sit on the sofa, she in the middle and Jackson and me on either side of her.

Jackson takes her hand. "Ava, don't worry. Luke is a smart guy. He'll be fine."

"Luke just felt like it was the right thing to do, Ava," I say. "He believes it's his responsibility to make sure you and the baby are okay now that Mick is gone."

"Doesn't he realize I'm quite capable of taking care of myself and this baby?" She looks down at her belly.

"I don't believe he's thinking clearly," I tell her. "It's not that he's underestimating your ability. Luke is still mourning Mick."

"I suppose you're right. He and Mick were so close, but Luke didn't cry at the funeral. I just realized he's never cried. No wonder. He was so busy taking care of me, consoling his parents, handling all the funeral arrangements, taking me to my doctor's appointments, and getting us ready to move to Dallas." Ava's eyes widen. "Oh my God, Trace. We took advantage of him. He hasn't had a chance to grieve."

"No, he hasn't. Taking care of you and his parents was his choice, Ava. It allowed him to escape and not to face what actually happened to Mick. He's pushing his feelings deep down inside." *That's something I definitely can identify with.*

"Now that reminds me of Mick, always worried about me and others more than himself. Luke is so much like Mick." She sighs. "Sometimes it's hard for me to look at Luke. He and Mick were identical in more ways than just their appearance. Even their gestures were the same. I barely could tell them apart but was always able to. They loved trying to trick me, pretending they were the other one. I can't tell you how many times they would change into each other's shirts thinking they would fool me. I always went along with it, even though I was never fooled, just to hear them laugh."

Listening to Ava talk about how Luke was with his twin breaks my heart. He lost so much. So did she. I would have loved to have met Mick.

"Mick and Luke were so carefree. But Luke has become so much more serious since the accident. He has got to know I would never marry anyone without love. And that's a long way off for me. I'm still mourning too. I do love Luke, but he's my brother. I don't want him sacrificing everything for me and my baby. Yes, I need him to be a part of my little boy's life. That's what Mick would have wanted too. But to get down on his knee and ask me to marry him? It's crazy."

"I know it sounds crazy, but like I said, he feels totally responsible for you and the baby. He told me so. Maybe it's because he and Mick were twins. I've always heard there's a special bond between twins."

"That was so true with them. They were inseparable." Her eyes fill with tears.

I try to console her. "I can only imagine how tough it's been on both of you. Luke may be going about this wrong, but his intentions are honorable and good."

"Thank you for saying that. I know his heart is in the right place. He's a wonderful guy. And so are you, Trace." She turns to me and smiles. "I've seen how he looks at you. I've never seen that look on him before."

"That's funny," Jackson says. "I've never seen Trace look at anyone like he does Luke either."

A loud, hard knock at the door shakes the windows and startles us.

"What the hell?" Jackson says as I get up to answer the door.

Ava sighs. "I'm sure it's Luke."

I open the door and see she's right.

Luke is standing in front of me, red faced, with his hands curled into fists by his side. He looks past me to Ava. Then his eyes return to me. "At it again, I see. Just like with Sarah and Martha. Butting in to things that aren't any of your business."

"Luke, I don't—"

"But you do. You did. You're the reason Ava turned me down. I can see that now. You got in her head before I got to ask her, didn't you?"

"No, I didn't. I swear."

"Don't give me that crap."

I hate how upset he is but don't know what to do about it. His whole plan just went up in smoke. He has to be crushed, feeling like he's let down his brother.

Ava leaps off the couch and steps between me and Luke. "Lukas

David Wagner, first of all, no one got in my head about anything. I have my own mind. Second of all, I had no idea Trace even knew you were going to ask me to marry you until after you already had. I just found out when I came over here that he knew about your plan. Third, I know you're hurting but please stop being an ass."

I'm amazed and impressed at her tenacity. But I'm worried about Luke. It's clear he's reeling with emotions.

Ava takes both Luke's hands. "I'm not a porcelain doll without any brains. I have plans of my own. For me and my baby. Does that mean you are excluded from my plans? Not at all. I want Mick's and my baby to know his Uncle Luke. He's going to be so lucky to have you in his life. You will be a fantastic uncle. I know Mick would be so proud of you and grateful for all you've done and continue to do for me and the baby. But I also know your brother would never expect or want you to give up everything. We've been through hell together, you and I. And we survived."

"Maybe you survived, but I'm nothing but a fuck up." And without another word, Luke turns and bolts out the door.

"I've got to go after him," Ava says. "He can't live with guilt like that."

As she runs out the door, Jackson and I glance quickly at each other. No words are spoken. Not necessary. We know what we have to do, and we follow her.

I see Luke sit down on the bench next to Malcolm's tree. His face is red and his eyes are closed.

Ava stops several feet away from him as we come up beside her. "Let's give him a moment, guys. It's time he grieved for his brother."

I know she is right and we stay back a respectable distance. Except for the four of us, the courtyard is empty. I hate what he's going through.

After several minutes, Luke opens his eyes and we walk over to the bench. Ava sits next to him and takes his hands once again.

He kisses her on the cheek. "I'm sorry, Ava. I obviously didn't think this through. There's a suffocating emptiness inside me, a hole that won't go away. I wish I'd been the one who was in that car when the drunk driver hit Mick. If I hadn't called Mick that night to help me with Mr. Knight's new calves, he would still be alive."

Through tears she says, "Luke, I had no idea you were suffering with that kind of guilt. You can't blame yourself. Mick loved helping you. You know he drove out to the Knight Ranch to be with you at least three or four times a week. Nothing happened for years. It was just an accident. That drunk driver is to blame, not you."

"I felt like if I would do something for my brother, the pain would go away. But it's not going away. Nothing is helping."

"Buddy, it may be a cliché but it's true," Jackson says. "It'll get easier with time. I know. Believe me, I know."

I realize Jackson is talking about his mother, who died tragically last year.

My heart is aching for Luke. "I can't imagine what it feels like to lose someone so close to you. What I do know is I'll be there for you if you need me. I don't care what time of day it is, Luke. Just let me know if you want to talk or just don't want to be alone. Whatever. I'm here for you."

Luke's eyes fix on me. "No matter what I do I can't seem to get over losing my brother. The whole world changed when he died." A single, lonely tear falls from his eyes and rolls down his face.

It's clear to me Luke's about to lose it. He needs to. It's the only way he's going to be able to start the healing process. So I sit down on the bench and put my hand on his shoulder.

Luke looks at me with the saddest eyes I've ever seen.

I want to help him more than anything. "You need to listen Ava. You have to know that accident wasn't your fault. You can't blame yourself for a drunk who got behind the wheel when he should have given his keys to someone sober. That wasn't your decision. There wasn't anything you could have done to change what happened, but what you can do now, is honor your brother by living your life and continuing to be the kind, wonderful man you are."

He closes his eyes and wraps his arms around me, facing the loss of his brother head on.

Chapter 9

M ockingbird Place's courtyard is packed with people for Oliver and Adam's wedding. There's at least two hundred in attendance. Of course every resident is here. We are like family after all. There are also members of the Rainbow Student Coalition, several professors from the university, and more.

I'm so thrilled that Chief Torres, who leads the campus police department, is sitting with his wife and son in the place of honor where the parents' sit on Oliver's side. He and Oliver are very close.

Right behind the chief's family sits S & M, both of them with happy smiles but holding handkerchiefs for their coming waterworks.

Our local trio Red Shimmer, minus Franki, is playing a soft melody as the rest of the guests take their seats. Franki and Candy are maids of honor, Oliver and Adam's two witnesses. It's still strange seeing Chad and Josh alone without Franki, but I'm starting to get used to it. Franki moved in with Candy a couple months ago. I worry the band will eventually break up because of it. I hope not, but I'm so happy how madly in love Franki and Candy are.

The courtyard looks incredible, but I knew it would because of

Oliver's decorating talents. Every chair is tied with a wide blue bow. Along the center aisle are white and blue rose bouquets attached to the chairs. He and Adam are getting married under Malcolm's tree, which has paper lanterns in all the colors of the rainbow hanging from its branches. Though the colors Oliver and Adam chose are blue and white, they wanted the multi-colored lanterns to acknowledge how grateful they are for the Supreme Court's ruling. I'm still amazed that Oliver and Adam's marriage will be recognized in all fifty states, including Texas.

I sit next to Ava, but most of my attention is on one very handsome usher—Luke. He's been so kind since the talk under Malcolm's tree with me, Ava, and Jackson, but we've seen no smiles on his face.

"Is Luke doing any better?" I ask Ava.

"A little."

"I know he needs time to process what he went through the other night. I only hope he's dealing with his grief in a positive way. I don't want to see him slipping back into that dark depression he's suffered with since his brother's death."

"I agree. He had his first appointment with a grief counselor and has two more scheduled for next week."

"I'm thrilled to hear that. Going to a counselor shows he's taking the steps to move forward. I've been through counseling myself. It's hard work but I know he can do it."

"You really do care about him, Trace."

"Yes, I do," I confess. "Enough to give him whatever space he needs, but I have to be honest. I was hoping he would call me by now."

She smiles. "Don't worry. He will. Trust me."

"I really hope you're right."

She grabs my hand. "I am right. Just try to be patient." Her eyes close. "Ohh."

"What's wrong?"

"Little Mick is doing a cartwheel. Want to feel him?"

I nod, in awe that she has a new life inside her. Luke's nephew.

She places my hand on her stomach.

"Wow, Ava. I just felt him kick."

"The little devil is keeping me up at night running laps. I'm so ready to have this baby. My due date is two weeks from today, but the doctor says it could be any time."

With a grin, I say, "I hope the baby waits until after the wedding to introduce himself."

"So do I."

Adam's granddad takes his place under Malcolm's tree, waiting for the two grooms to walk down the aisle between the chairs. He's officiating the ceremony. "Please, everyone turn off your cell phones. Thank you." The man has such a commanding voice. I can visualize him leading his troops back in Vietnam.

As Red Shimmer switches into the wedding march, Candy and Franki come out of Unit A, arm in arm, carrying blue and white corsages. Candy wears a blue dress. Her long brown hair is accentuated with a white ribbon. Franki's black hair is spiked and she has on a white tuxedo with a blue tie.

After the two women take their places under the tree, we all stand. Oliver and Adam come out of their apartment with Adam's mother, who is escorting them down the aisle. Adam is dressed in a blue tuxedo with a white tie and Oliver is in a white tuxedo with a blue tie.

I can't remember ever seeing Oliver so happy. He and Adam are all smiles.

Once they are at the end of the aisle, Adam's mother kisses both of them and then takes her seat. The grooms move forward, Oliver standing next to Candy and Adam next to Franki.

Adam's granddad has tears running down his face. "We are gathered here to witness a momentous occasion, the marriage of Oliver Lancaster and Adam Stockton." The man's voice shakes and he wipes his eyes. "I can't tell you how happy this makes me. Adam is my grandson and hero. Oliver is also my family, a grandson of my heart. He, too, is one of the bravest men I've ever known. I love them both so very much."

We're all so moved hearing the old Marine express his feelings about Oliver and Adam.

"Gentlemen, please take each other's hand."

The two handsome grooms turn to each other and clasp their hands together.

"Oliver and Adam, we are so thankful that the United States government now recognizes your commitment. Your friends and loved ones are here to celebrate the public expression of love you are giving to one another. I understand that you wrote your own vows. Adam, we'll begin with you."

Adam smiles, his eyes fixed on Oliver. "If it wasn't for you I wouldn't be standing beside you right now. You helped me to face my doubts and embrace my true self. You're the most courageous man I know. Life with you is so much more than I could ever hope for or imagine. I choose you to be my husband, and I offer myself in return. I will care for you, stand beside you, and share with you all life brings our way from this day forward, and all the days of my life. I love you, sweetheart."

Oliver brings out a slip of paper. "Adam, from the moment you dropped that box on the sidewalk the day you moved into Malcolm's apartment, I was a goner. We both had issues we had to work through, and with each other's help we did. I never dreamed I would find someone so amazing as you to spend the rest of my life with. I'm so thankful you came into my life. You've given me everything." Oliver looks at Adam's mom. "A mother." He turns to Adam's granddad. "A grandfather." Then his full attention returns to Adam. "And yourself. You don't hold anything back. You shower me with love. I can't wait to be married to you, to be your husband. I promise not just to grow old together, but to also grow together. I love you with all my heart, Adam. Now and forever."

As Oliver and Adam exchange rings, I glance over my shoulder at Luke, who is standing with Tony, the other usher. It seems like Luke is mesmerized by what is happening under Malcolm's tree.

"By the power vested in me by the state of Texas and supported by the Constitution of the United States of America, it gives this old grandpa and ordained reverend the great honor to pronounce you, Adam Stockton, and you Oliver Lancaster *Stockton*, legally married."

Everyone comes to their feet and applauds.

Ava grabs my hand and squeezes. "I didn't realize Oliver was going to take Adam's last name."

"That doesn't always happen, but in Oliver's case he not only gets Adam, he gets a new family. That's why he took Adam's last name."

Adam's grandfather smiles. "Now, boys, you may kiss each other."

Oliver and Adam kiss and everyone cheers once again.

For a second time, I glance back at Luke. Our eyes lock for a moment and then he turns to Tony and says a few words. They walk to the parking lot. I remember that they are in charge of decorating Oliver's car. Jackson and I are supposed to help them along with Hayden, Eli, and Jaris.

I wonder what Luke is thinking right now. Could he still be upset that Ava turned him down? I sure hope not. I wish I knew.

As Oliver and Adam march down the aisle as husbands, Ava moans.

"Are you okay?" I ask, taking her hand.

"I'm not sure. Probably nothing."

"Do you want to go back to your apartment?"

"And miss the reception? Absolutely not." She smiles and then immediately frowns. "Oh boy. I don't think little Mick wants to go to the reception."

"Another pain?"

She nods. "I don't want to make a scene, Trace. Do you mind helping me walk back home?"

"No, and then I need to get Luke."

"Maybe I can call him." She pulls her phone out of her purse. "He might have turned his phone back on. Nope. Voicemail. Luke, when you get this message, please call me."

"I think I should call 911, Ava."

"No. I'll be okay. I've read that a mother can be in labor for hours and hours with their first baby. There's plenty of time. Ouch."

"Something tells me there isn't plenty of time. Let me get Jaris." I scan the crowd for our resident doctor, Jaris Black, who lives in

Unit H, but I don't see him. "He's got to be around here somewhere."

"Trace, please. I just want to get home."

"Okay, Ava. Maybe we'll see the doc on the way to your place." Unfortunately, we don't see Jaris as we walk to her apartment.

Once inside, I ask, "Do you want to lie down?"

She shakes her head. "I just want to sit at the table for a minute."

Holding on to her, I lead her to one of the chairs.

She sits.

"Better?" I ask.

"Much better. Thanks for helping me get back to the apartment." She looks at me. "Do you think anyone noticed we left? I don't want to ruin Oliver and Adam's big day."

"Nobody noticed. Besides, how could you ruin their wedding? We are all so excited about little Mick. Even if you had the baby today, Oliver and Adam would be bragging about him being born on their wedding day. That would be the best present you could give them. And of course, everyone else would be thrilled too."

"I hope you're right, but even if I'm in labor it's likely going to be tomorrow. Some women have gone up to twelve hours...oh God. Oh God. That was the worst one." She lowers her eyes. "Damn."

"What's wrong?" I ask, full of worry.

"My water just broke."

"That's it." I run to the door, open it, and yell, "Dr. Jaris Black, we need you ASAP in Unit E! Now! And Luke, wherever you are get your ass in here. Your nephew is coming."

The entire crowd turns my way and the music stops.

Sarah is standing steps away from the door and rushes inside past me to Ava.

I run back in and lift her off the chair. "I don't know what I'm supposed to do."

"You need to carry her upstairs," Sarah says. "I'll get some towels for the bed before you lie her down."

"They're in the linen closet," Ava tells her.

As I start up the stairs with Ava in my arms, I ask, "And then I'll start boiling the water?"

She grins. "That's not necessary. That just happens in the movies. Oh. Oh. Oh. Damn."

Sarah grabs an armful of towels, and I hear more people walk into the apartment.

"Trace, I'm here," Jaris says.

"Where is Ava?" Luke's tone is frantic.

"We're upstairs, guys," I yell down.

Sarah lays out the towels and turns to me. "Ready."

Gently, I lower Ava onto the bed and another pain hits her.

"It hurts so bad."

Jaris enters the bedroom. "Apparently you didn't get the manual, Ava. You're supposed to be in labor for several hours, but I guess your baby has other ideas. Don't worry. I've done this many times. I'll take good care of you. Tony is getting my medical bag out of my apartment."

Sarah places a sheet over Ava's legs. "Bend your knees, sweetheart. I need to raise your dress and pull off your panties."

"Oh God. I have to push, Doc," Ava yells.

As Sarah tosses her panties aside, Jaris turns to me and Luke. "I need hand sanitizer, stat."

"I've got some in my pocket," I say, reaching in and pulling it out.

"Pour it on my hands, Trace."

"Doc!" Ava's voice is louder than I've ever heard it.

Luke rushes to her side and takes her hand.

After Jaris finishes sanitizing his hands, I move to the head of the bed and take Ava's other hand. My heart has never pounded faster in my life.

"Oh. Oh. Oh."

"Push, Ava," Jaris tells her. "That's good. Okay, breathe."

"I'm here, Doc," Tony yells.

It seems to me that everyone's voices have gone up several decibels.

"Bring it to Ava's bedroom," Jaris says. "Okay, Ava. You ready? Bear down and push again."

Ava groans loudly as Tony walks in backward with Jaris's medical bag.

"I see the baby's dark hair. One more push and your baby will be here."

Sarah takes the bag from Tony. The MMA fighter immediately rushes back downstairs.

I feel Ava squeeze my hand tight as she groans and closes her eyes. The next thing I hear is a baby crying.

Jaris smiles. "You have a healthy baby boy, Ava. I would say he's a seven pounder, at least."

Jaris hands the baby to Sarah. "Luke, would you like to cut the cord?"

Luke's face is filled with love. "Is it okay, Ava?"

"Yes."

In total awe of what I am lucky enough to witness, I continue holding Ava's hand as Luke cuts the cord.

Chapter 10

As Luke and I walk out of Ava's bedroom together, I say, "That was the most amazing thing I've ever experienced in my life."

"Same here. God, I'm so glad you were sitting next to her when she went into labor." For the first time since the talk under Malcolm's tree, Luke is all smiles.

Once downstairs, we see that all our neighbors are anxiously waiting to hear the news.

Luke announces, "Mother and baby are doing fine."

Everyone claps.

"That's great news, Luke," Hayden says and hugs his wife, Lashaya.

"I only hope I make it to the hospital before our baby comes," she says.

Hayden and Lashaya live next door to Oliver and Adam and are expecting their first baby in about seven months. Malcolm took them in when her parents disowned her for marrying a white guy.

"Martha, Doc and Sarah asked us to send you up to help get Ava and the baby ready for visitors," I tell her.

"My pleasure." Martha rushes up the stairs as Jaris comes downstairs.

"My job is finished," he says to Luke. "She's in good hands with S & M. I have to get to the hospital for my rounds. Who is Ava's obstetrician, Luke?"

"Dr. Thornsberry. I have her number in my phone."

"I know Emily Thornsberry. I'll call her and let her know about the delivery. Call me if you need anything at all."

"I will." Luke hugs him. "Thank you so much, Jaris."

"No thanks needed. This is why I became a doctor." He turns to Oliver and Adam, who are still in tuxedos. "Congratulations, guys. Sorry I have to run."

"We're just glad you were able to make the ceremony," Oliver says. "And deliver Ava's baby. Hell, Jaris. You're a superhero in our eyes."

He laughs. "Nope. Just a doctor."

Jaris leaves.

Oliver and Adam step up to Luke and shake his hand.

"Congratulations," Adam says. "How is the proud uncle doing?"

"Never better. Congratulations to the two of you."

Oliver smiles. "We were hoping to see Ava and the baby before going back to the reception."

"We'll make sure you are the first to see her."

I take a seat next to Jackson. He and Eli are sitting on the sofa together. I swear those two have something going on.

Jackson leans over to me and asks, "So how does it feel to have witnessed a baby being born?"

"Not just any baby. Ava's baby. How does it feel? I can't even find the words to describe it. It was unbelievable. It was wonderful. It was…a miracle. I won't ever forget it. Jackson, I know this sounds crazy, but I just love that baby. How is that possible? How can you feel so much for someone you essentially just met?"

"I'm not sure."

Eli leans forward. "Let me see if I can help answer your question. I actually had to deliver a baby for a woman my first month as a fireman. It's very possible to feel so strongly right away. Like you said, Trace. It's a miracle. Elisa, the mother, and I still keep in touch and I go visit Jason all the time. He turns two next month." Eli laughs. "He calls me Unkey Lee-Lee. Isn't that cute?"

Jackson smiles.

"It sure is cute." I get tickled seeing that strong fireman have such a soft side and how Jackson is reacting to him.

Harvey comes through the door, holding some blue roses. "Is little Mick here yet?"

Oliver laughs. "Harvey, I'm amazed you were able to get flowers so quickly."

He grins. "Well, son, you're married now, so I figured you and your new husband wouldn't want your flowers to go to waste. They can be from all three of us."

Adam says, "How very thoughtful of you, Harvey."

We all roar. Everyone is joyous and thrilled with our new arrival at Mockingbird Place.

Martha comes down the stairs. "Okay, listen up. Ava wants to see all of you, but here are my rules—only two at a time and keep your visit short. A couple minutes each. Oliver and Adam, you go first. I'm sure you need to get back to your guests."

I'm not surprised by Martha's take-charge attitude. We do need a leader right now, and she's like a mama bear protecting her cub when things get crazy around here. And I can't remember a time that was ever crazier than today.

Everyone follows her orders to the letter—two at a time and two minutes max.

The last to go up the stairs to see Ava are Jackson and Eli. The rest have gone back to the reception, leaving Luke and me alone downstairs.

I look at Luke and a strange feeling comes over me. It's like we're a family. Me. Him. Ava. And little Mick. I know I'm jumping the gun but I can't get over this feeling. I remember what Ava said about raising the baby on her own. She's very capable. But I can't shake this. It's just weird. I wonder what Luke is thinking.

Martha leads Jackson and Eli down the stairs.

"He's the cutest baby I've seen in my life," Jackson says to everyone.

Eli grins. "That baby is a miracle and so is his mom."

He and Jackson shake Luke's hand and walk out the door together.

Martha sighs. "Ava is a trooper. She's tired and needs her rest, but she's insisting on seeing you two. Please keep it short."

"We will." Luke hugs Martha. "Thank you. We couldn't have had this baby without you and Sarah."

"Of course you could. Babies come on their own time."

I hug her too. "You and Sarah are the best, and we're just glad you were here."

"Me, too, and yes, we are the best." She grins. "Now go."

Luke and I rush up the stairs and see a very tired Ava holding the baby.

Sarah hugs us both. "Keep it short, boys. M's rules, you know."

"We know," Luke and I say together.

"I'll be right downstairs if you need me." She leaves, closing the door behind her.

"Would you like to hold him?" Ava asks us.

Again, we answer in unison, "Yes."

"Luke, you go first," I say.

He nods and takes the baby from Ava. "Hi, little Mick. I'm your Uncle Luke. Your daddy and I were brothers. He would have been so proud of you."

I put my arm around Luke and can almost feel his mix of happiness and sadness swirling inside him. Even though he's a tough cowboy, I see tears in his eyes. I look over at Ava and see tears in her eyes, too, which makes my eyes tear up as well.

Luke breaks the spell saying, "Aren't we a bunch of marsh-mallows?"

We laugh and cry at the same time.

"Your turn, Trace." Luke places the baby in my arms, and again I get that strange feeling, only it's even stronger.

"Hey, little guy." Seeing him yawn fills me with joy. "Big day today. Happy birthday to you. I'm so happy you're here and your mama is letting me hold you."

Ava smiles. "I had a reason I wanted to talk to you together. It's about the baby's name. What do you think about me naming him Michael Lukas Trace Wagner? We would still call him Mick though, unless he's been bad, and then we would call him by his full name."

Stunned, I say, "I'm so very honored, Ava."

"I think it's a great idea." Luke puts his arm around my shoulder and stares at the baby. "Hey, cowboy. Uncle Trace has been a hero to your mom and me."

"A hero? What do you mean?" I ask.

"Twice you've saved the day, Trace."

"Twice?"

"Yes. When Ava collapsed, you were right there to take us to the hospital."

Trace smiles. "I'm glad I was."

"And then today, when she went into labor, you came to her rescue. Damn right, you're a hero." He touches the baby's cheek. "Hi, Michael Lukas Trace Wagner."

I can't remember ever being so happy. "Do you think he'll like the name Trace?"

The baby starts crying.

"Oh no. He hates that name," I say, handing him back to Ava. "Is he okay?"

"I don't know. Maybe he's wet or hungry? Call Sarah and Martha up here. I don't want to make a mistake."

I run to the door and yell, "S & M, get up here. The baby's crying."

They rush in the room, and Luke and I step back.

Sarah takes the baby from Ava. "This little guy needs a diaper change." She quickly changes him but he keeps on crying. Handing him back to Ava, she says, "He must be hungry."

"What do I do?" Ava looks at S & M. "What do I do?"

"Um, I'm not sure," Martha says. "We've been around our fair share of newborns but we've never been present for a baby's first meal."

Ava turns to me and Luke. "Google it?"

"Google what?" we ask in unison.

"Breastfeeding, of course," she says anxiously.

We both pull out our phones.

"I got it," Luke says. "How to start breastfeeding. The first time you hold your newborn is a great time to start breastfeeding."

"Get on with it." Ava is beyond antsy. "Just the important stuff, Luke."

"I don't know what's important." He starts reading really fast. "Your body will produce small amounts of a special milk called colostrum that will help protect your baby from infection."

"I don't care about that. He's crying. Get to the point."

I hold up my phone. "Here's a video I found on a site called Breastfeeding Wonderland that we can watch."

"Oh my God. Play it."

I hold my phone so Ava can see and we all gather around.

We watch for a few seconds, and Ava says, "Pause it, Trace. Pause it."

"Okay."

The image freezes on the woman lifting her naked breast.

"I think this is right." Ava lifts up her blouse and exposes one of her breasts.

Luke and I turn our heads.

"Guys, I don't care if you look. It's just a boob and you two are gay. It doesn't matter. And frankly, I need help. Turn the video back on, Trace."

"Yes, ma'am."

The announcer's calm British voice says, "Place the areola in your baby's mouth and wiggle it until your baby latches on. It may take a while. Don't be impatient."

"Pause it." She follows the instructions. "Wow. He's doing it already."

"That's amazing," Luke says.

I smile. "I'm not surprised. Michael Lukas Trace Wagner is a genius."

Chapter 11

I watch Jackson finish wrapping the last of the gifts we bought for the baby shower. I'm the *sous*-wrapper to him and he is the *chef*-wrapper, which I don't mind. His giftwrapping skills are exceptional. I'm more of a gift bag kind of guy, stuffing tissue paper around the presents. And Jackson? He could work full-time at Neiman-Marcus wrapping presents during the holidays for customers if he were so inclined.

"Hand me a piece of tape, Trace."

"Here you go. They all look terrific. Great job."

"Thanks." Jackson spins the last box around. "Do you think we went overboard with the gift buying for little Mick?"

"Absolutely not. In fact I have a couple more things I'm going to pick up to give Ava after the shower."

Jackson puts away the wrapping paper, scissors, and tape. "You're nuts about that baby."

"I sure am. I just can't explain it. Something happened to me being in the room when he was born. And when I first held him I was hooked."

"That's called bonding, buddy. You're over there ever waking hour of the day. But I guess I would be too if Ava had named the baby after me."

I smile. "Not just me. Luke and his brother, too."

"I still can't believe Ava is going back to class tomorrow. She just delivered the baby on Saturday. She's a toughie."

"Yes, she is. Ava thinks she'll have to drop classes if she misses any more days. She's very focused on staying on her plan to get her degree. Luke and I tried to convince her to take the entire week off, but we couldn't change her mind."

"Speaking of Luke. How are things going between you two? Better I hope."

I shrug. "I don't know. Yes, better, but we've both been so focused on Ava and the baby these last three days, we haven't had any time to talk. I never realized how much you have to know to take care of a baby. I figured just a diaper change and putting a bottle in his mouth, but there's much more to it than that."

"How many diapers have you changed?"

"I don't know. The three of us are splitting that duty. Quite a few, that's for sure." I look at the time on my phone. "We have an hour before the baby shower."

"I better get over to S & M's for the surprise. They wanted my help with some of the decorations."

"I'll see you there."

Jackson walks out the door with the rest of our gifts, and I head upstairs. I want to get cleaned up before I head over to Ava and Luke's place. Since the baby arrived earlier than expected, we decided to have the shower on Tuesday instead of Saturday. She's completely in the dark, believing we're going to S & M's for dinner with the baby. I can't wait to see her face when we walk into Unit I and everyone in the complex is there for the shower.

I strip out of my clothes. Before turning on the faucets in the shower, I can't help but place my ear to the wall wanting so badly to hear Luke sing again. But of course I can't hear anything. Harvey repaired the wall, replacing the sheetrock and tile already.

As I wash off, I start humming the song that Luke and I shared when the wall was much thinner between our places. The two of us are getting along great, but Jackson's question keeps rolling around in my head. "How are things going between you two?"

I'm still holding onto hope that he's interested in me more than just as a fellow diaper changer. Yes, we're friends. I have no doubt about that. But if I'm being truthful with myself I have to admit I want more. He's an amazing person. So kind and loving. Loyal and sincere. Funny and so very sexy. But does he want more? I just don't know.

He went to his counseling session this morning and came back all smiles. I'm thrilled he's working on his feelings of loss for his brother. But is he ready to start dating? Should I wait for him to ask me out or should I make the first move?

As I rinse off, I decide I'm going for it. I will ask him on a date. Come what may, I want at least a chance with Luke. One date. It's a start. I finish cleaning up and get dressed.

When I go downstairs, I lift the cover off of the canvas and look at the painting. It isn't finished yet but it's going so much faster than any other painting I've ever worked on before. Why wouldn't it with Luke giving me such inspiration? I'm happy with how it's turning out. I've never painted a Western scene until this one. I still need to finish shading the wild horse with the flaring nostrils, but the cowboy in the saddle is complete. Luke's intense brown eyes in paint move me. I wonder if he would like it.

I trust him. I trust him more than anyone. But can I find the courage to show him this? I'm not sure. Maybe after a few dates I could? Perhaps.

I place the cover back over the painting. It's time for me to go over to Unit E.

When I step out of my apartment, I notice the lights around the pool are on. The days are getting shorter and shorter. Soon the holidays will kick into gear. I look forward to the decorating of the courtyard with my neighbors, which happens every year the first weekend of December.

When I ring Unit E's doorbell, it takes all my willpower to hide my excitement. I don't want to ruin the surprise.

Ava opens the door and gives me a hug. "Come inside. Luke is changing the baby. We will be ready to leave as soon as he's finished."

"You look fantastic." I step back to get a better look at her. She's wearing a pretty blue dress. "I can't believe you just had little Mick. Your figure looks perfect."

"Far from perfect, Trace, I can assure you. But thanks. My doctor gave me some exercises to do and I've already started on them."

"It's working, but I hope you have room for a big meal because S & M are both great cooks." What Ava doesn't know is they've been preparing a huge buffet for all the baby shower guests since early this morning.

"Actually, I'm starving. I only had a bowl of fruit for breakfast and a salad for lunch to make room for their delicious meal."

Luke comes down the stairs holding little Mick. "Guess who's here, sweetie? Your Uncle Trace." With a subtle wink, he hands me the baby. "All clean and ready."

I kiss little Mick on the forehead. "Shall we go?"

"Yes," Ava says.

Luke goes over to the door and opens it for Ava, me, and the baby.

I am so happy we've been able to keep the party secret from Ava.

It's only a few steps to S & M's apartment. Ava rings the door-bell and Luke and I move back. He looks at me and smiles. God, he is so good-looking. I smile back.

Sarah opens the door. "Come inside."

Ava enters and everyone jumps out of the hiding places and shouts "Surprise!" and starts taking pictures with their phones. She steps back and covers her face with her hands.

I'm so glad that I'm holding the baby and not her. Hopefully someone got her picture before she covered her face. "Be sure to send me copies of those photos."

"Me, too." Luke pats me on the back.

Grinning, Ava shakes her finger at us. "You two tricked me."

"I think everyone tricked you, sweetheart," Luke says. "We were all in on it."

"So I see. You're all a bunch of sneaky devils."

Sarah puts her arm around Ava. "Would you rather eat or open presents first, honey?"

"If you don't mind, I'd like to eat. Everything smells delicious."

Sarah leads her into the kitchen. "This your baby shower and buffet. As guest of honor, you are at the head of the line. We have fried chicken, ham, pot roast, and for the vegetarians among us, we made spinach stuffed Portobello mushrooms."

"This is so sweet of you." Ava's eyes widen as she views the expansive spread. "I'm not a vegetarian but may I have one of the stuffed mushrooms? Sounds delicious."

Martha comes up beside her. "However many you want, sweetheart—one, two, or three. It's your party. Where is that precious angel?"

"I've got him, but I'm willing to share." I hold him out for Martha.

She takes the baby in her arms. "Oh my goodness. He's so adorable. Someone take our picture quick."

Tony and Hayden are the first two to jump up and snap several shots of her holding the baby, but everyone else crowds in like paparazzi a second later with their phones out.

"Okay, you guys." Sarah holds up her hands like a traffic cop. "Would you please let Ava have a plate? She's hungry."

Martha hands the baby back to me. "You heard the lady. Let's make a line."

Seeing S & M take charge in their loving yet firm way makes me smile.

"May I hold the baby for a second?" Lashaya extends her arms. Hayden is standing next to her. On the other side of her is a good-looking guy I've never met, but the family resemblance between him and Lashaya is obvious.

"Of course." I pass little Mick to her.

"So cute. I hope my baby and you will become best friends."

"Trace, this is, Brexton, Lashaya's younger brother," Hayden says. "Brex, this is our good friend, Trace."

I shake hands with him. "Nice to meet you. You and your sister look so much alike."

"Thanks. Nice to meet you, too." There's sadness in his eyes that can't be missed. I wonder what caused it.

"Brex is moving in with us." Lashaya passes the baby back to me. "He's going to start classes next semester."

"Awesome. You're going to love it, Brex. If I can help, just let me know." I can tell there's more to his story than what she's saying.

Luke comes up beside me. "I'll fill my plate, and then I'll take Mick from you so you can fill yours."

"There's no need for that," Franki says with Candy next to her. "We can help out."

Candy smiles. "Plus, we all want a chance to hold this sweet boy. May I, Trace?"

"Sure. Thank you."

Luke and I go into the kitchen with the rest of the crowd.

"Wow. Look at this spread," Luke says. "S & M made enough food for an army."

"They always do." I start filling my plate to the max and glance back at the baby, who is now being held by Oliver and Adam.

The newlyweds are back from their two-night honeymoon in Taos, New Mexico. Oliver and Adam couldn't go longer because of their classes, but they plan on taking a vacation in the summer.

After the meal, several of us help S & M with the cleanup, which takes no time at all.

As Jackson wipes down the last counter, Sarah says, "Everyone to the living room. It's time to give Ava her presents."

There are not enough chairs for everyone, so many of us take our seats on the floor, like Luke and I. It's nice that he's stayed next to me during the party. Yes, I'm still going to ask him out on a date. *Right after this party.* Thinking about that makes me nervous wondering what he'll say.

"Ava, you sit in my chair." Martha smiles, pointing at her over-stuffed recliner. "This is the place of honor."

Sarah nods. "M and I will hand you your presents. Leave every-thing to us."

"But before that, we have a game we want to play that S and I call Blindfold Diaper Change. The one who changes it the fastest and correctly will get a nice prize." Martha lifts up a bottle of wine.

Holding a stopwatch and a doll, Sarah shakes her head. "M, you weren't supposed to show that until someone won."

"I just wanted them to try their best, and what better motivator than a bottle of wine?"

Everyone laughs.

"Let me go first." Chad raises his hand. "I want that wine. Actu-ally, I need that wine. I got a B on a test today, and I'm in a grumpy mood."

We all laugh. Chad is never in a grumpy mood. He's always the life of the party.

Josh puts his hand on Chad's shoulder. "Okay, go first, but I don't think that's a good strategy. Better to see how everyone else does it and then go."

"Maybe so, but I still want to go first." Chad downs the rest of his drink. "Bring on the blindfold and the baby, ladies."

Once S & M have him in position, Martha yells go and Sarah starts the stopwatch.

Chad leans forward, frantically lifting the doll by its feet.

"You don't lift the baby by its feet," Franki yells out.

"Thanks for the tip." He lays the doll down on the coffee table backward, with its head closest to him and the legs the other direc-tion. "This is the first diaper I've ever changed."

"We can tell." Josh laughs and we all join in.

When Chad places the diaper on the doll's head, everyone roars.

"Done." He raises his hands above his head.

Sarah clicks the stopwatch. "Thirty-two seconds."

"That's good. Better than I thought I would do."

"S, we weren't going to give out the times until everyone goes. Remember?"

"I forgot, but I don't think it will be a problem on this one. Chad, you can remove your blindfold."

Once the blindfold is off, he says, "I'm suffocating the baby." He looks at Ava. "You're never going to let me watch little Mick now."

She grins. "Sure I will, but we will have some diaper changing lessons without a blindfold."

I'm the last to try my hand at the game. When I take off the blindfold, all eyes are on S & M and the notepad they wrote all of our times on.

"Well?" Ava leans forward in the chair. "Who won?"

"Actually, we have a tie," Sarah says. "The best time was twelve seconds. Both Luke and Trace are the winners."

Chad smiles and mockingly folds his arms over his chest. "Not fair. They've had lots of practice changing diapers."

Luke slaps Mockingbird Place's imp on the back. "And so will you, buddy."

"So will we all." Harvey holds the baby. "We're all here to help you with little Mick, Ava."

"No truer words could be spoken, Harvey," Martha says.

Eli nods. "That's for sure."

Several others share the same sentiment.

"I don't know what to say." Ava smiles. "I'm overwhelmed. Luke and I have only lived here for such a short time and you've embraced us with open arms. You're family to me now. Thank you."

"Seems like you do know what to say, sweetheart." Martha hugs her. "And very nicely put. We love you. You are family to us, too."

I watch as happy tears fall from Ava's eyes. I can't imagine what it must have been like growing up in foster care for her. I'm so glad that we are here for Ava—her new family. I don't have any brothers and sisters of my own, but she is my sister of the heart in every way possible. She means the world to me.

"Hey, guys. Should we have Trace and Luke draw straws to determine the final winner?" Candy asks, lightening the mood.

"They should arm wrestle for it." Chad grins. "With their shirts off."

We all laugh.

"Sorry, Chad. That's not necessary." Luke puts his arm around my shoulder. "Trace and I can share the title and I have an idea about how we can enjoy the wine together."

Luke's words surprise me. "You do?"

He nods and smiles. "I'll tell you about it later."

As Ava opens the presents, all I can think of is what Luke's idea is for us about sharing the wine."

Chapter 12

On the third and final trip back to Luke and Ava's apartment, he and I carry the changing table that Lashaya and Hayden bought. Hayden and his brother-in-law Brex, Oliver and Adam, and S & M are with us, taking the final batch of gifts from the baby shower to their home. Everyone else is back at Unit I, putting away the dessert dishes, cleaning up, and taking out the trash. I still can't believe how massive the pile of wrapping paper was.

Ava is already inside with Lashaya. The two of them went on ahead to get Mick ready for bed.

"Our little guy and Ava got quite the haul tonight," Luke says as Martha opens the door for us.

We take the piece up to Ava and the baby's room. Mick is asleep and she and Lashaya are sitting on the bed talking.

They look up at us.

"Where do you want this?" I ask Ava.

"Next to the window, please."

The rest of the gang walks in with the remaining gifts.

"Just look at all of this. I won't need to buy baby clothes or anything else for months."

Sarah smiles. "That was the plan all along. And don't worry, sweetheart. Just because the shower is over doesn't mean that M and me won't be buying more for that precious baby boy of yours."

Ava stands and hugs S & M. "Thank you so much."

"We love you," they say in unison.

"I love you, too."

Martha turns to us. "Okay, guys. Time to go and let Ava get some sleep. She and the baby need their rest."

"And don't forget, M," Sarah says. "Ava is determined to go to class in the morning."

"I can't forget. I'm so proud of her. And Luke, if you need any help with that baby call us."

"I will. Thank you. But I think Trace and I can handle it."

Martha grins. "Perfect. Okay, sweeties. Goodnight."

As we walk downstairs with the others, Luke says quietly to me, "Stay for a bit. I want to talk to you alone."

"Sure." I'm anxious to hear what he has to say about sharing the wine. Plus, sticking around after everyone leaves will give me a chance to ask him out on a date.

I sit down on the sofa and listen to Luke tell everyone good-bye.

He locks the door and plops down next to me. "Whew. That was fun but I'm exhausted."

"Me, too, but I can't imagine how Ava must feel." I turn up the baby monitor and we hear both mother and baby breathing softly. "Thank God they're both asleep already."

"I don't want her to have to get up during the night, so I'm going to take care of the baby. There's three bottles of breast milk in the refrigerator that Ava prepared earlier, so she should be good until morning."

"I'll get here by seven to take care of the baby so you can sleep while she's in class." I glance at the bottle, which is on the coffee table. "Congrats on winning S & M's baby shower game."

He smiles. "We both won, Trace."

"Yes, we did. So what is your idea about the wine?"

"I was thinking it was about time you and I went on a date."

I'm overjoyed. "Great minds think alike. I was intending to ask you out too."

"So I assume your answer is 'yes' then?"

"Definitely it's yes."

He presses his full, manly lips to mine. I melt into him, and it feels so right. It's like we've been together forever.

When he releases me and leans back, I stare into his gorgeous eyes. "Luke, that's the best kiss I've had in my life. Honestly."

"Unlike our first one when you thought I was straight and with Ava?" He laughs.

I kiss him back. "Yes. Much better."

"I was thinking we could have dinner Saturday night. Do you know any BYOB places where we could take our prize with us?"

"I sure do. Do you like Thai food?"

He shrugs. "I've never had it before. Is it like Chinese? I love Chinese."

"It's similar in some ways. I'm sure you'll enjoy it."

"Good. It's a date. Seven?"

"If you don't mind, how about six instead? That way we can beat the dinner rush and won't have to be gone long from Ava and the baby."

"That's a great idea. Six it is." Luke leans back. "I'm glad we're going out, Trace. Really glad."

"Me, too. We sure started off funny, didn't we? Seems like everything was against us."

"Yeah, but now we can put that aside and start again." He smiles. "I know what Mick would say if he were here."

"What would he say?" I ask.

"He never gave up on anything in his life. He loved this quote by Harriet Beecher Stowe. 'When you get into a tight place and everything goes against you, till it seems as though you could not hang on a minute longer, never give up then, for that is just the place and time that the tide will turn.' "

I hug him. "Your brother was not only handsome, but very wise too."

"Yes, he was."

87

We stay wrapped in each other's arms as Luke reminisces about Mick. Some of the stories he shares make me laugh. Others make me smile. And still others make me cry. But all of them are worth listening to and make me feel even closer to him.

We talk on and on, eventually falling asleep on the sofa together.

Little Mick's cry coming through the monitor wakes us, and we both leap from the sofa and run up the stairs.

Thankfully, we find Ava still asleep.

I pick up the baby, and as quietly as I can, say, "Grab the diaper bag, Luke."

He nods, and we tiptoe out of the bedroom, which makes me smile. "Quite the opposite in how we came up the stairs, don't you think?"

"We sounded like a herd of cattle."

"Only a cowboy like you would come up with that comparison."

"I was in a deep sleep when the baby's crying startled me. I'll warm up the bottle if you'll start changing him."

"You bet." I take the diaper bag from him. "I'm sure this is going to take longer than twelve seconds."

"Really? You're not even blindfolded, Trace."

I love his sense of humor. "You just take care of the bottle and I'll handle the diaper changing." I look at the baby. "We got this, don't we?" I place him on the sofa and pull out a diaper and a baby wipe from the bag. When I remove the wet diaper, the floodgates open up and Mick baptizes me. "Shit." I hold the clean diaper over him.

"Don't curse in front of the baby, Trace."

I grin. "Like he understands me. I just got soaked."

Luke comes out of the kitchen with the warm bottle. "You know he has a tallywacker."

"Tallywacker? God, you are a cowboy through and through."

"I sure am. Let me take over and show you how it's done."

"Be my guest." I step back.

"How's my cowboy?" Luke removes the diaper I'd been holding over Mick and he gets doused just like I did. "I thought he was done."

We both start laughing so hard it's difficult to catch our breaths.

Still in hysterics, Luke says, "Remember we don't want to wake Ava."

"Right. Shh."

"Where is he getting all that pee?" He pulls out another clean diaper.

"I guess his tallywacker wasn't finished yet, Luke," I say, which throws us into another round of laughter.

After ruining two clean diapers, we finally get little Mick cleaned up and ready for his bottle.

Holding the baby in my arms, I place the bottle's nipple in his mouth. "Let me show you how this is done." I start singing "Rock-a-bye baby."

Luke starts laughing again.

"Hey, I'm not that bad of a singer, am I?"

"That's not why I'm laughing. I'm laughing because I see this tiny baby has this big strong man wrapped around his finger."

"You're one to talk, cowboy."

Luke puts his arm around me. "That's *fer* sure. Ain't it wonderful," he says, thickening his drawl.

Ava comes down the stairs. "I heard so much noise. Is the baby okay?"

"Yes, sweetie," Luke says. "I'm sorry. We should have been quieter. We didn't mean to wake you. We just got tickled because little Mick drowned both of us."

"How in the world could he have drowned both of you?" She grins. "Do I need to search for a video on changing a baby boy's diaper to show you?"

We smile and tell her what happened.

She starts giggling, and Luke and I lose it again. "Where's your phone? I want to get a picture to put in the baby book S & M got me to immortalize this special moment."

Luke hands her his phone.

"Go sit by Trace," she tells him. "Now. Each of you hold up one of those diapers and look at little Mick. Perfect." She snaps a couple. "Now one with me in the shot." She crouches down in front of us. "Say 'pee.' " She takes several more shots.

As we continue laughing, the emotion from the day the baby was born returns—only stronger. I look at little Mick, who is sound asleep, and then into Ava's and Luke's eyes. This trio feels like my family. I can't wait to introduce them to Mom and Dad. I know they're going to love each other.

Hold on, Trace.

I haven't even been on a date with Luke yet. One thing at a time.

Despite my attempt to rein in my thoughts, suddenly a ball of pressure builds inside me. If I screw up my date with Luke, I could ruin everything. What happens then? Will they still want me around? I can't imagine living my life without them in it.

The date must be perfect.

Chapter 13

Sitting in a quiet corner of the restaurant and enjoying our soup, I can't believe how wonderful my date with Luke is going. "So how's the job search?"

"I forgot to tell you. I got a job as a hand at a horse ranch that's forty minutes up US 75 or an hour in traffic."

"When did you interview? I've been with you almost every second since little Mick arrived."

"A rodeo buddy of mine is the foreman's cousin. He gave me such a glowing recommendation that the foreman called and offered me the job over the phone. I told him about little Mick and Ava and that I didn't want to start right away. The guy said he had no problem flexing my schedule. I'll be on the payroll the first of next month, but he told me I could drop by anytime to get familiar with the facility and the other hands. He even said I could bring Ava and any other friends."

"That's terrific, Luke."

"I'm just glad to have a job I know something about. I wouldn't be good at a desk in an office building." He smiles. "But being outdoors, building fences, breaking horses, and anything to do with ranching…those are things I do know a thing or two about and enjoy."

"I've never been around horses or cattle before. I'm a city boy, a native of Dallas."

"Mm." Luke rubs his chin. "I'll have to get you in the saddle soon. I think you'll love it."

An image of Luke and I horseback riding appears in my mind. "I bet I will love it."

"Native of Dallas, huh? Your family live in the area?"

I nod. "Mom and Dad's house is about twenty minutes from Mockingbird Place. They live near White Rock Lake."

"What do they do?"

"Mom's a physical therapist and Dad owns a landscaping company. He's like you. Loves the outdoors. You'd get along well with them."

"I'm sure I would. You seem like you're very close to your parents."

"I am. They're the best. They've done so much for me." I think about how wonderful Mom and Dad have been my entire life— especially how loving and understanding they were after I told them about what happened to me in junior high.

"It sounds like both of us have wonderful families." He smiles. "I'm so excited for you to meet Mom and Dad. They're going to love you."

"My parents are going to love you too. We are both very lucky."

"Yes we are. I can't wait for them to arrive. They love Chinese food as much as I do. And I'm pretty sure they'll love Thai as much as I do now."

I'm so happy he likes the food. "What do you think of the place?"

"I feel like I'm in Southeast Asia." He motions to the wall with the mural. The scene is very intricate and features a small village in Thailand. "That's very nice. And so big. I wonder how long that took to paint."

"Two months. The owner's sister painted it. She and I are in a couple of classes together. Very talented artist."

"Yes, she is."

"She's having a showing of her work at the campus next week. Maybe we could make that our second date?" I smile, hoping he'll say yes.

"Are they serving wine?" He winks at me, and a tiny tingle shoots up and down my spine.

"Yes, I believe so."

"Then it's a date, though by then we'll have been on at least two or three more. Right?"

"At least that many, not counting my coming over and seeing you, Ava, and the baby."

"I love it when you come over. The door is always open for you. In fact, Ava and I have talked about giving you a key to the place."

That familiar feeling of connection with them and the baby washes over me. "Would Ava be concerned about her privacy?"

"Apparently not. She suggested it. Besides, it's not like she's walking around the apartment in the nude. And you've already seen her breasts." He laughs.

I grin. "You're evil, Luke."

"Sometimes." He finishes his *tom kha* soup. "Trace, I would love to see some of your paintings."

My gut tightens, thinking about my painting of him. I'm almost finished with it. "I don't show my work, Luke."

"You don't? Ever? Why not?"

I shrug. "I know it sounds strange, but it's a quirk of mine."

He frowns, clearly confused. "Don't you eventually want to make a living as an artist after you finish college?"

"Most artists have to work other jobs and their creativity is a sideline. More than likely I'll teach art or curate for a museum."

"But is that what you want to do?" Luke's question is straight and to the point.

"No. I'd like to be a full-time artist," I confess, but I'm not ready to tell him why that's an impossible dream. "It's complicated." Hoping to change the subject, I ask, "Do you like the soup?"

"You bet I do. Delicious." He takes a sip of his wine. "Our prize is good too. Are you sure we can't have two glasses instead of one? We could Uber back to Mockingbird Place."

I'm relieved that we are no longer talking about my art. "I think we better put a cork in the bottle and stow it in the trunk when we leave. We can finish it back at your place. Besides, aren't we still stopping at the mall to get the baby and Ava presents?" We both know it's silly to continue buying them gifts, but we just can't help ourselves.

"Yes, we are definitely going to the mall."

The waitress brings the dishes I ordered for us. She refills our water glasses and takes away our empty soup bowls.

"I'm so glad you ordered for us. This looks delicious. Which is the pad thai?" Luke asks.

I point to the noodle dish. "And the other one is laab. Let me warn you that both dishes are spicy."

"I like spicy." He smiles broadly. "I'm the kind of guy who wants extra jalapenos with my Mexican food."

"Then you'll love this."

He takes his first bite of the pad thai. "This is good. And what did you say the other one was called?"

"Laab. L-A-A-B. It's pronounced like…I'm going to *lob* the ball to you. It's a cold, savory dish."

"Cold? Interesting." He gets a forkful of it. "I like this even more. Yum."

"I'm so glad you are enjoying them. The secret is in the sauces."

He reaches across the table and grabs my hand. "I'm having fun, Trace."

I squeeze his hand back. "So am I."

After a few more bites, my phone rings.

"Is that Ava?" Luke asks anxiously.

"I don't recognize the number. Hello?"

"Congratulations. You have won a trip for two to Hawaii," a recorded voice tells me. "Please remain on the line for—"

I click off my phone. "Telemarketing call."

"I thought it might be Ava," he says, which doesn't surprise me.

"I can't stop thinking about her and little Mick either. Why don't we box up the rest of this and head home?"

"We're acting like two overprotective uncles, Trace. Are you sure you don't mind cutting our date short? I'm having a blast."

"Hold on, Luke Wagner. Who said anything about cutting it short? We are just going to hit the pause button. Once we get back to your place we'll spend some time with Ava and the baby. When they go to bed we'll go sit by the pool and continue our date with the rest of the wine. Deal?"

He nods. "Deal. I'm sure we'll have more fun when we know they're okay."

"Yes. Because I know we're both worried since this is the first time they've been alone."

"Let's still stop by the mall on the way back. I don't want to come home empty-handed."

I grin. "Neither do I. But what can we get them? Do you have something in mind?"

Luke places the cork in the wine bottle. "I thought we could get Mick a mobile for his crib. For Ava, I thought we could stop by Cheri's."

"Cheri's?"

"Yes. She loves their bath products. All we have to do is tell them that her favorite scent is jasmine and they will make up a basket for her."

"I didn't know she likes jasmine. She always smells very good." I wonder what else I don't know about her or about Luke.

"I didn't know either until Mick told me. He would buy it on occasion for her. There's our waitress."

I wave her over.

"Yes, sir?"

"Could we get these boxed up and get our check, please? We're in a bit of a hurry."

She smiles. "Of course."

After she leaves the table with our plates, I gaze at Luke's warm eyes. They have gold flecks that I want to make sure I capture in my painting.

The waitress comes back with our boxes and our check.

We both grab the ticket, and neither of us lets go.

"I insist, Trace. This is my treat. I asked you out first."

"I didn't realize you could be so stubborn."

He grins. "You have no idea."

"Okay, if you promise to let me get the next one." I let go of the ticket and pick up our food.

He pays for the dinner, and we walk out.

Once inside Luke's truck, he leans over and kisses me, making me warm all over.

"Your kisses just get better and better."

"Let me try another one and see if I can improve." Luke presses his lips to mine, deepening our kiss. He then stares at me with his piercing sexy eyes and wicked, devilish grin. "Well?"

I try to catch my breath. "Mm. Let me think about it." I pause for a split second and then blurt out, "I don't know how it's possible, but yes, it was better."

"I could stay here and kiss you all night, Trace."

"We better not." I laugh. "I don't want to attract a crowd in the parking lot. Besides, we better hurry if we're going to stop by the mall."

"Damn it. You're right." He starts the engine and drives us to the mall.

We rush to the baby store.

"What do you think of this one, Luke?" I point at a mobile with tiny horses, cows, and chickens hanging from a red barn.

"It's perfect for our cowboy."

We run to Cheri's. The sales lady has a basket ready in no time at all, and then we are on our way back to Mockingbird Place.

Once in the parking lot, we are both so excited to get back to Ava and the baby to give them their presents that we run all the way to the door.

She's sitting on the sofa holding little Mick. "What are you two doing back so soon?"

Luke bows. "We have gifts for thee and the prince, my lady." He pulls the mobile out of the bag.

"Guys, that is so adorable. You've already bought so much. You didn't have to do this."

"Yes we did have to do it." Wanting to follow Luke's example, I also bow. "And this is for thee, my lady. We traveled to the Far East to acquire fragrances." I wink, handing her the basket. "Actually, North Park Mall."

She giggles. "It is east of here, my lord. I love it. How did you know I like jasmine?"

"Luke remembered Mick giving you bath oils and salts with that scent."

Handing me the baby, her eyes well up but she still smiles. "Thank you both so much." She opens her arms wide, wrapping them around Luke and me.

"Little Mick's asleep," I tell them. "Let me put him to bed, and I'll be right back."

Ava nods and kisses me on the cheek.

Once upstairs, I kiss the baby as I gently lower him into his crib. "Sweet dreams," I whisper softly.

I stand there for a few moments, gazing at the baby. God, I love him. He's stolen my heart. I'm so happy to be a part of his life. He's got his whole future in front of him. I see his innocence and vow to never let anyone steal it from him like mine was.

I make sure the monitor is on before leaving the room.

As I descend the stairs, I hear Luke and Ava laughing. When I step into the living room, I find them sitting on the sofa with a laptop in front of them.

"Trace, come over here," she says. "You've got to see this."

"See what?" I sit next to Luke.

She points at a picture on the screen of Luke and his brother dressed up as medieval knights. "I took this picture of Luke and Mick at our high school football Halloween bash."

"God, you two do look identical," I say to Luke. "I can't tell which is which."

"I'm the knight with the red feather. Mick has the blue one." Luke clicks the arrow on the screen and a picture of Ava in a princess costume pops up.

She sighs. "I wonder if I'll ever be able to fit back into that outfit again."

"Sure you will," he says and turns to me. "Ava loves Halloween. It's her favorite holiday."

"Mine is New Year's."

He laughs. "You two are so much alike. Those are weird holidays to top a list. I know she likes Halloween because she gets to dress up in costumes. But why do you like New Year's best?"

"I don't know. I guess it's because it is the one day of the year I consciously let go of all my doubts, fears, and regrets. It's the place where the past and the future intersect, and I feel like there is nothing but possibility in front of me."

"Wow." Ava smiles. "I think you made me see New Year's in a totally different light. It's not just about resolutions you're going to break in less than a month or two. It's about dreams and new beginnings. Very poetic, Trace."

I shrug. "I don't know about that, but it's how I feel."

"Ava is right. You are poetic." Luke puts his arm around me. "You're an artist and a poet."

"Multi-talented. That's me." I laugh. "Show me more pictures. Please."

Ava nods and brings up the next photo. It's of the three of them on horseback. "This was my seventeenth birthday party. Luke was in charge, as you can tell."

As we look at more photos, it becomes quite clear how in love Ava and Mick were. It's also very obvious how close Luke was to his brother and to Ava. He and Ava are still very close, maybe closer because of sharing the same loss. There is so much history between them.

As they continue to share their memories with me through tears and laughter, I begin to wonder where I fit in to their family. Doubt crawls out of the dark depths inside me, clawing its way to the surface. I just found out that her favorite scent is jasmine. What else don't I know? What if the sense of connection I've felt since witnessing little Mick's birth is nothing more than a delusion, a lie— a figment of my overactive imagination? Do I even belong here?

With them? With little Mick? But more importantly, do I belong with Luke?

Am I just being crazy?

I don't know. What I do know is that I'm in deep and if I don't get out soon, I'm sure to drown.

Chapter 14

When Ava says goodnight, I kiss her on the cheek, feeling the weight of this good-bye like it is a million pounds. "Sweet dreams."

"You, too." She gives Luke a hug. "Night."

"I'll take the four o'clock feeding, Ava," he says. "I want you to get some real rest tonight."

"That would be wonderful. Thank you."

"You're welcome. Trace and I are going to sit by the pool for a bit, honey. If you need us just call."

"I'm sure the baby and I will be fine. See you in the morning." She smiles at us. "Love you both so much."

"Love you, too," we say in unison.

She yawns and goes to her bedroom.

Luke gets two wine glasses out of the cabinet and grabs our bottle off the counter. "Ready to hit the 'play' button on our date?"

My doubts tug at me. "I don't know, Luke."

He looks confused. "I don't understand."

I wish I knew what to say to him, but I'm also confused. I haven't been able to get rid of the apprehension I'm having. All those pictures we looked at earlier prove how connected Luke and

Ava are to one another. Even though I feel so close to them, is it even possible for them to feel that close to me? They're family. I'm not. And the three of us just met a short time ago. "It's getting late, Luke."

"What do you mean it's getting late? Neither one of us has to get up early? Tomorrow is Sunday."

Needing time alone to figure out how I fit in to his and Ava's situation, I hold up my phone to show him the time. "Actually, it's already Sunday."

"So? I don't care what time it is. I just want to be with you." He gives me a light kiss and opens the door. "Come on. Let's go. No arguments." He grabs my hand.

"Is that an order?" I smile, as my fears back down a little. Another kiss from him, and they are in full retreat.

"You could call it that if you'd like. I'm just not ready for the night to end yet."

"Me either," I admit, despite what little remains of my worries. I wrap my arms around him and stare into his eyes. Then I step back and give him a mock salute. "Private Trace, reporting for duty, sir."

We walk out to the bench under Malcolm's tree.

Luke fills a glass and hands it to me. "Trace, we were having such a good time and then suddenly your mood seemed to change. Did I do something wrong?"

"No. It's not that. You didn't do anything wrong. You've done everything right."

"Then what is bothering you?"

"It's hard for me to answer that."

He puts his arm around my shoulder. "I'm here for you, Trace, and I'm ready to listen to whatever is on your mind."

"I know you are. Seeing all those photos of you and Ava and Mick got me to thinking. We don't know that much about each other."

He smiles. "That's the beauty of a new relationship, sweetheart. We get to discover more along the way."

I take a big gulp of wine for courage. "Being open has been difficult for me for a very long time, Luke, but there's no one more than you who I want to be open with and to know the real me."

He refills my glass. "I want that too, Trace."

I take another sip and close my eyes, letting my mind drift back into that dark place. "I was twelve years old when it happened."

JIMMY THROWS the football to me and I catch it, racing for the end zone.

"Run, Trace," Coach Shultz yells from the sidelines. "Show us what you got."

Wanting to make him and all my friends proud, I run as fast as I can. I can't believe I made the football team. Seventh grade is turning out great so far.

Alvin, who is thirteen and the biggest one on the field, tackles me on the five yard line, slamming me to the ground and knocking the wind out of me.

I can taste the grass and dirt in my mouth as I try to catch my breath and keep from crying. The next thing I know, Coach Shultz is lifting me off the ground and to my feet.

"You okay, Trace?" He puts his hands on my shoulders.

Standing, I choke back my tears and nod. "Fine…I'm…okay."

Coach Shultz turns to Alvin. "What the hell is the matter with you? This is just a scrimmage. I told you older boys to take it easy on the new kids this week, didn't I?"

Alvin is nervous and looks down. "Yes, Coach. I just got into the play. I'm sorry."

"You should be." Coach Shultz looks at the rest of the team. "Everyone hit the showers."

They all race to the locker room, but Alvin doesn't move. Is he in trouble?

Hoping to smooth things out between him and Coach Shultz, I say, "I'm okay, Coach. Good hit, Alvin."

Alvin smiles.

Coach Shultz puts his arm around Alvin, and the smile vanishes. "Go. It's okay. We'll talk later."

Alvin looks at me in a weird way before racing to the locker room.

I take a step to follow, but Coach Shultz moves in front of me.

"Not you, Trace. Not yet. You and I are going to gather up the equipment and put it away."

"Yes, sir."

By the time we are done, the other boys are out of the showers and dressed.

"Take a seat, team." Coach Shultz walks over to the white board and begins writing out the practice times for the rest of the week. "I'll see all of you on the field in your uniforms at four o'clock tomorrow for another scrimmage. Don't be late. Now, get out of here."

As Coach Shultz finishes filling out our schedule on the white board, Alvin says to me. "Trace, want to get a Coke with me and Jimmy and some of the other guys before heading home?"

"Sure. Sounds fun." I feel like part of the team now.

Coach Shultz comes up behind me. "He'll have to take you up on that offer another time, Alvin. I can't let one of my football players leave without a shower, and Trace hasn't had one yet."

Alvin shakes his head. "We'll wait."

"No, you won't," Coach Shultz says firmly. "Get out of here. I want you rested for tomorrow's scrimmage."

I'm so disappointed that I have to stay. I want to go with the other boys, but don't let on to Coach Shultz.

"Trace, hurry," Alvin says. "Meet us at McDonalds."

"I will. Thanks."

He and the others leave.

I stand, go to the showers, and strip off my clothes. I plan on showering as fast as I can so I can meet Alvin and the others.

I turn on the faucets.

"Hold on, Trace."

"Okay, Coach." I cover my dick with my hands, nervous about being naked in front of Coach Shultz.

He puts his arm around my shoulders, giving me a strange feeling. "I'm glad you're on my team. We need a nice boy like you. But you're new. You've never played on a team before, have you?"

"No sir, but I have played with my friends."

"Playing with friends and playing on a real team is very different. There's so much you need to learn. You're very lucky that I'm here to teach you." Coach Shultz starts to undress.

I'm scared to death. Why is he doing this?

"Trace, the first thing I'm going to show you is the right way to take a shower."

When I see the evil look on his face, I know I'm in trouble.

"COACH SHULTZ STOLE MY INNOCENCE."

I trust Luke and want him to know everything about me, so I tell him the rest. How Coach Shultz molested me that night. How I ran all the way home, forgetting about Alvin and the other boys at McDonalds. About the shame and confusion that swirled inside me with every step. How I buried my head in the pillow, wishing I were dead.

Being with Luke is opening me up completely. My walls are down.

"Few people know this story. My counselor. My parents. Jackson. But I've never shared as much about that horrific day with anyone like I'm sharing with you right now."

"I'm glad you trust me." Luke's caring eyes are filled with tears. "My God, Trace. How horrible that must have been for you. I'd like to beat the shit out of that monster right now."

"That's what my dad wanted to do, too, when he found out. But he didn't get the chance. I was terrified to face Coach Shultz. I convinced Mom and Dad I was sick for two days and was able to stay away from school and the football field. On the third day when I begged to stay home again, my mom said 'I don't know what is going on with you, Trace, but I do know that you are not really sick. So you will sit there until you're ready to tell your dad and me what's going on.' I lied, saying everything was fine. She wasn't fooled and reminded me that no matter what my secret was, she and my dad would be there for me. I don't know how long it took, though it felt like forever at the time, but eventually I broke down sobbing and told them what Coach Shultz had done to me."

"What did they do?"

"They hugged me and said that everything was going to be okay. What none of us knew was that Coach Shultz was dead. The night before, the bastard passed out behind the wheel of his car and hit a tree head-on. The coroner's report said he had a heart attack. It was all over the morning news, and everyone was hailing Coach Shultz as a wonderful man and amazing teacher. I never went back to that school, never saw the other boys. Mom and Dad were great. Everything did get better. They pulled me out of that school and put me into counseling. That's when I started painting. It was part of my therapy. Still is."

"That's why it's hard for you to share them with other people."

"That's right." I take another sip of wine, trying to put my thoughts together. "Luke, I've never gotten real closure. The fucker died."

Luke grabs my hand. "I can't imagine how hard this has been on you, but please believe me, Trace. I'm here. With you. You're not alone. We'll figure this out together."

"Together? After looking at those pictures with you and Ava, I'm not sure where I fit in. You two are so close, and I'm—"

"You're the most amazing man I've ever met, and Ava loves you like a brother. And little Mick needs his Uncle Trace. Hell, he has your name. You fit in just fine with us. And with me you're a perfect fit." He leans over and kisses me.

For the first time in my life, I feel like I have a chance for true love.

"Look what I still have." Luke pulls a key out of his pocket. "Want to join me in Unit F?"

Filled with warm emotions, I smile. "I sure do. Let's grab a bottle of wine and a blanket from my place first."

We walk into the apartment, which is totally dark. Quietly, so as not to wake Jackson, I get the things we came for and we leave. I feel a bit giddy and a whole bunch wicked.

Luke unlocks Unit F's door and we go inside. Once the door is shut, our hands are all over one another. Heat rolls through me like a bonfire. Our kisses are wild and full of passion.

"God, I want you. I want you so much." His tone deepens and electrifies me.

Filled with desire, we race to unbutton each other's shirt. I run my hands over his muscled chest and torso, relishing in the feel of his body.

He kisses my nipples, bathing them with his sinful tongue, which drives me wild. We spread the blanket out over the floor and lie down side by side, exploring each other's body with our mouths and hands. I can't get enough of him. The more I touch and taste Luke, the more I want and need him.

I unbuckle his belt, unfasten the button, and unzip his jeans. He's wearing black briefs, and I can see the outline of his cock under the fabric. I grab him and he groans. He's massive and so very hard, which fuels my desire even more.

I pull down his jeans and briefs to his ankles and lick my way up his legs back to his thick dick. I cup his heavy balls and circle my tongue on the head of his cock.

Another hot groan escapes Luke's lips and I feel his hands on the back of my head. "Feels so good, Trace. So very good."

I swallow him and lightly squeeze his balls. Loving the impact I'm having on him, I suck him, going up and down his shaft.

"Damn. Oh God." Luke is vibrating like a live wire. "Close, Trace. So close."

His words enflame me and I double my tempo, wanting to taste his cream.

He groans, tugging on my hair.

I feel him shoot into my mouth and I swallow every one of his drops. I'm thrilled that I could give him so much pleasure. I release his cock and before I have a chance to say anything, Luke flips around into a position on the blanket that places his hot mouth between my legs.

"My turn to get a taste of you, sweetheart." He removes my jeans. "Boxers. I like." Then he pulls them off of me, tossing them to the side.

When I feel his sexy mouth on me, I lose my mind. "Oh. Oh. Oh God. This feels so good. Wow."

He doesn't lose his rhythm, bobbing up and down my cock, despite my groaning and writhing under him. His lips dragging against the shaft and his tongue swirling on the tip multiplies my need for release.

"Going to come, Luke. Can't hold…can't hold…ahh." I shoot down his throat as the explosion erupts inside me.

I roll over on my side.

Luke moves behind me, wrapping his arms around me and kissing the back of my neck. "That was wonderful, Trace."

"For me, too."

"You like to cuddle?" he asks.

"Never before now, but don't you dare let go of me."

"I won't." He nuzzles my neck. "Same for me. Never cuddled anyone before, but there's something about you that won't allow me to let go. I could stay here all night."

"But you promised to take care of the four o'clock feeding." I pull out my phone from the pocket of my discarded jeans. "It's already after three. We better go check on little Mick. You know he sometimes wakes up earlier than we expect."

"Just five more minutes."

"Five more sounds good to me." The doubt I had been feeling after looking at the photos with him and Ava is gone. I told him about my worst nightmare and he understood how that had plagued me all these years. Lying in his arms, I feel so close to him, not just physically. It's much deeper than that. It's like a bond has been created that links us to each other—a bond that seems unbreakable.

"Trace?"

I roll over on my side, facing him. "Yes?"

He smiles. "I'm crazy about you."

I kiss him. "That's funny, because I'm crazy about you too."

AS LUKE IS in the kitchen getting a bottle ready, I walk up the stairs to Ava's bedroom. She's still asleep and the baby is just starting to stir.

Grabbing a diaper and some wipes, I quietly lift little Mick out of his crib and carry him downstairs.

After I change him, Luke gives him his bottle. "So far, we've kept him from crying."

I can't help but smile. "We make a good pair, don't we?"

He nods. "In more ways than one."

I lean over and kiss him on the cheek. Why is it so easy with him? It feels so natural, like we've been on a thousand dates already instead of just one. "Ava is still sound asleep."

"Good. I hope since tomorrow is Sunday she can catch up on her rest. I'm going to try to convince her to have a pajama day, and I'll try to take charge of the baby if she'll let me."

"I'd like to help you."

"I wouldn't have it any other way." Luke kisses the baby on the forehead. "Looks like this cowboy is finished with his bottle." He puts the baby over his shoulder and begins trying to burp him. "Trace, it means so much that you trusted me with your story."

"It did lift a big weight off of my shoulders, but I still wish I'd been given the chance to confront the son of a bitch. I would have punched him in the face."

"Yeah. You didn't get the kind of closure you deserved."

The baby finally burps.

"Feel better?" Luke lifts him off his shoulder and carries him back upstairs.

God, I am falling in love with that man. I'm falling hard and fast.

When Luke returns and joins me back on the sofa, he puts his arm around my shoulder and I lean into him.

"Trace, have you ever been back to that school, maybe talk to the principal? Do you think he's still there?"

"No. I've never been back. I don't know if the same principal is at the school. At that time the principal was a woman. Principal Shirley Harris is certainly young enough to still be there. I would guess her to be in her early forties by now. She was always very kind to me. I liked her a lot. I always wondered what she thought happened to me when I never came back."

"Maybe it's time you found out," he says. "It might help you get a little closer to the closure you want."

"I have to think about that, but you might be right." I turn my head and lock eyes with him. "I know one thing for sure. It makes me very happy that you care."

He kisses me. "I do care for you, sweetheart. I care very much. And I want you to be completely happy."

"I want the same for you, Luke." I touch his face, thinking about the loss he's suffered. "And we can work on that together. But first, there's something I want to show you."

"There is?"

"Yes." I stand. "Come with me."

"Back to Unit F, I hope," he says with a devilish smile.

"Maybe after." I write Ava a note letting her know that we will be at my place if she needs us. "What I want to show you is in my apartment."

"Lead the way."

Once inside Jackson's and my place, I take him to the canvas, which is still covered. "God, I'm nervous to show you this."

He kisses me lightly. "Don't be. I would like to know what kind of things you paint."

I take a deep breath, still unable to bring myself to remove the sheet. "I'm taking this to my storage unit. That's where I keep the ones I've completed. I just finished this one so it's going into storage tomorrow. But I wanted you to see it before I put it away. God, I hope I'm doing the right thing. What if you hate it?"

"I'm sure I will like it. Show me."

"Here goes nothing." My hands are shaking as I slowly pull the cover off.

Luke takes my hands and squeezes, clearly trying to reassure me. His eyes widen, as he studies the painting. "I can't believe this, Trace. That's me. It looks just like me." He pulls me into his arms. "That horse is perfect. It looks exactly like Warrior, one of the first horses I broke. So realistic. Oh my God, is that Mick standing by the fence?"

"Yes. I felt like he had to be a part of this."

"Wow."

"You really like it?"

"God, yes. I love it," he says. "I remember you telling me about your quirk not to let people see your paintings. God, you don't know what it means to me that you showed me this one. Look at how you painted my eyes. It's as if you can see into my soul." Luke steps back. "Trace, I want this painting. Please, can I have it?"

Chapter 15

L ying in my bed, I stare at the ceiling replaying Luke's question over and over in my mind. *I want this painting. Please, can I have it?*

I told him I needed to sleep on it before I could answer and then we said goodnight. He went back to his place, and I tossed and turned all night.

What can I tell him? I shouldn't have shown it to him. That was clearly a mistake. Or was it?

My art has always been the only outlet that's worked to release my anxiety, especially when the past begins to suffocate me. What if I let him have the painting and this channel stops working? What if I go absolutely crazy because too many people will see my work and know what happened to me? My pain is in every brush stroke. My heart starts thudding hard in my chest.

I sit up on the side of the bed. "Get a grip, Trace. You're just working yourself into a frenzy for no reason."

Deep down, I know I should let Luke have the painting. It's past time for me to get over this. It's long overdue that I stop holding out for a closure that will never happen. Coach Shultz is dead. There's nothing I can do to change that fact. That's all there is to it.

But there actually is more to it. Luke is in my life now. We have a chance at something special. Hell, if I let myself go, I can imagine marrying him one day. Who knows? Better to imagine a life with Luke than to let my fears crowd in and push me into the darkness.

I get out of bed and walk down the stairs.

Jackson is making coffee. "You're up early."

"So are you, especially since it's Sunday and you don't have classes." I walk over to the painting and remove the cover. Luke's eyes stare back at me.

Baby steps. One at a time.

"Jackson, do you mind pouring me a cup and then coming to take a look at my painting?"

"Sure. Um. What did you say?"

My heart starts to race, but I've made up my mind. No looking back. Only forward. "I'd like a cup of coffee and would appreciate you taking a look at this painting."

"That's what I thought I heard you say, but—"

"Just come on before I change my mind."

"You got it." Jackson walks next to me holding two cups of coffee. He hands me one and then looks at the painting. "Holy shit, Trace, that's good. Wow. I knew you were talented just from the few glimpses I've caught of other pieces of yours but I had no idea you were this great. Do you realize this is the first time you've ever let me take a long, hard look at your work?"

"Is it?" I take a sip of coffee, hoping to steady my nervousness. It helps some.

"You know it is. Damn, there's no denying who this is. Luke. Looks just like him. Ever since you met him I can see the changes in you. And now this? Wow, buddy. This is amazing. Has Luke seen it yet?"

"Yes. Early this morning. He wants it, Jackson. I haven't been able to sleep wondering if I should give it to him or not. You know why I have trouble showing my work to anyone."

"Yeah. It's your therapy."

"What if I lose that?" I cover the painting back up, glad that I had the courage to show it to him.

"You've got to follow your heart. What's it telling you to do?"

"That's just it. I want to give it to him but I'm scared."

"Then tell Luke that, Trace." Jackson puts his arm around my shoulder. "Let him know why you're hesitant to give it to him. And if you do decide to go through with it and hand this over to him, I'm always here for you."

"I know." Feeling more relaxed about everything, I yawn. "You're my best friend."

"And you're mine too. Give me that cup. You look like you could grab at least a couple hours of sleep now."

"You don't have to twist my arm." I hand him the cup, which I only took a couple sips from, and then head back upstairs to my bedroom. My bed looks so inviting now, not the monster that it felt like earlier when I couldn't sleep.

I crash down onto the mattress and immediately start to drift off with images of Luke's eyes in my mind.

A KNOCK on my bedroom door jolts me awake.

"Trace, you've got company," Jackson says through the door. "Luke is downstairs and wants to see you."

"Tell him I'll be right there." I jump out of the bed, feeling excited. "Jackson, do we have any coffee left?"

"Yes, if you want to cut it with a knife. It's noon, Trace."

I open the door. "Noon? It feels like I just fell asleep."

"Nope. You got five solid hours. Why don't I make a fresh pot?"

"Please. That sounds great." I walk into the bathroom as Jackson goes back downstairs. I quickly brush my teeth and my hair. After checking my reflection and feeling satisfied with how I look, I rush down the stairs, anxious to see Luke.

He must have heard my steps because he turns around and our eyes lock.

I go over and wrap my arms around his waist. "Good morning, handsome."

"Not morning, Trace. It is already afternoon." He gives me a tender kiss. "I'm glad you got some sleep."

Looking in his eyes, I can tell he hasn't had much sleep. "Did little Mick keep you awake?"

"He sure did." He smiles. "Every time I'd go to lie him down he would wake back up. That cowboy didn't want to go to his crib. So I just held him and watched some television. But I'm feeling pretty good under the circumstances. At least Ava got to sleep through the night for a change."

From the kitchen, Jackson says, "I know Trace wants a cup of coffee. How about you Luke? It's almost ready."

"If I want to stay awake today, I better have several."

"We have plenty. Rough night with the baby?"

"You could say that."

Jackson walks in with a tray that holds a carafe of coffee, two cups, cream and sugar, spoons and napkins. "This should help you. I made it strong for Trace. I could tell he needed a boost."

"Thanks, Jackson." I pour the coffee into the cups, enjoying the rich aroma.

Luke nods, adding cream to his cup. "This is great. Thanks."

"You're welcome. Guys, I would hang around but I am supposed to meet up with my study group. We have a huge test tomorrow." Jackson is so transparent.

I know his study group meets at five on Sundays, so he could stay longer if he wanted to. It's obvious that he's leaving early to give Luke and me a chance to be alone.

Grateful for his thoughtfulness, I say, "I'll clean up the kitchen."

"Perfect. See you two later." Jackson walks out the door.

Luke and I sit down on the sofa.

I look at him and take a deep breath. "Luke, I've thought a lot about giving you the painting. And although I really want you to have it, to be honest the idea of giving it to you scares the hell out of me."

"I don't understand. Is this about your quirk of not showing your work to other people?"

"Yes, but it's so much more than a quirk." I explain to him how my counselor got me to start painting as part of my therapy. "Even after I stopped going to her, I kept on painting. It helps when the bad memories haunt me. My art is how I cope with not having real closure from what that bastard did to me. Each piece is very personal. I can lose myself in my paintings, but showing them to others terrifies me. It's almost like when someone sees my paintings they can also see my scars, my pain, and the deepest, darkest parts of myself. I know it may sound crazy, but showing anything I've painted exposes all of me. Am I making any sense?"

"You're making a ton of sense." He takes my hand and squeezes it. "I'm sorry I asked for the painting. I didn't know how hard that would be for you."

"But I want you to have it."

"That means so much to me. And if there is any way I can figure out how to get closure for you, I'm going to find it."

I lean forward and kiss him. His determination is very special to me, though I know that closure will never be mine. "Like I said, I want you to have it but do you mind keeping it under your bed or in a closet for now? I have to take baby steps. That's the best I can do."

"Hey, it's okay. I don't mind putting it under my bed, and I promise no one will see it but me until you're ready. Baby steps are fine, Trace."

I take his hand and we walk over to the easel. I remove the painting, leaving it covered, and hand it to him.

He kisses me. "We'll take this as fast or as slow as you need. I know this has to be hard for you. I'm blown away that you trust me with this."

"Before I met you I didn't care if anyone ever saw my paintings. But now I want to show you everything I've painted because you understand me."

"God, Trace. I would be so honored to see all your works."

Filled with a sudden burst of courage, I ask, "How about now?"

He grabs my hand, and we walk out the door.

AS I PULL my car into the parking lot of the climate control storage unit facility, Luke calls Ava. He tells her we'll be back later and to call if she needs us.

When I remove the lock and raise the storage unit's door, Luke and I step inside. I flip on the light, illuminating the artwork boxes, each holding one of my paintings.

Surprisingly, I don't feel nervous at all. "This will take a while, Luke, if you want to see all of them."

"Unless Ava calls, we have nothing but time. Let's go for it."

I open one of the smaller boxes first. "This is my very first painting. My counselor asked me to name all of them. This one I named 'Alone and Afraid.' "

I lift the eleven by fourteen inch painting out of the box. Memories of what I was feeling at the time come rushing back in. In the middle of a stormy sea, a sailboat is being tossed back and forth. A single man in silhouette tries desperately to navigate the boat through the angry waves.

"Your very first painting? My God, there's so much meaning in this." He puts his arm around my shoulder and gazes at the painting. "How old were you?"

"Twelve."

"God, you were even talented then. This is fantastic. You're the man in the boat."

"I am. *Was.* I felt so alone and hopeless when I painted this."

"I can see that, but you weren't totally without hope. Look where the sailboat is heading, Trace. To the lighthouse on the shore."

"Oh my God, I never realized that before." I stare at the tiny ray of light I'd painted long ago. Luke is helping me see this painting in a new way. "I know when I worked on this it did help me calm down and the nightmares subsided. That's why I keep picking up the brushes. This is the first time I've ever been excited to share my pieces with anyone. I'm actually anxious to show you more."

Every painting we look at together, he's able to see things that I wasn't even aware of.

The last painting I show him is of a lion chasing a gazelle. I stare at the monstrous eyes and sharp teeth of the predator.

"You're the gazelle. The lion is that bastard who hurt you."

"That's right. That's what I was feeling when I painted this." Looking at my paintings again is difficult, reminding me of how lost I felt.

"But the lion hasn't caught the gazelle, Trace." He points at a section of the painting. "And look, you have it jumping over a stream. The gazelle is going to escape, just like you did. You made it past the stream. That fucker is dead and you're alive and well."

"Alive. Well. *And happy.* God, Luke. This is the best therapy I've ever experienced. I never saw the hope in any of my paintings before. But you did and helped me see deeper into myself—into what I was feeling. I wasn't totally lost."

"No, you weren't. You were strong. You *are* strong. You're incredible, sweetheart."

"So are you." I put the painting back in its box. "That's the last one. You've seen them all."

Luke puts his hand on my shoulder. "So, how do you feel after showing me all of your work?"

"It's the best I've felt in years since that monster attacked me. You have no idea how much you've helped me. You opened my eyes and let me see my paintings in a new light." My doubt and fear about my work begins to melt away. "What do you think about me showing them to other people?"

"I think that's a wonderful idea. Let's start with Jackson, S & M, and Ava. That way you can get a sense of how you feel about it before you show them to the world. Like you said before—baby steps."

I smile. "God, you understand me so well."

"Just like you do me."

We wrap our arms around each other and press our lips together in a passionate kiss.

Chapter 16

Walking out of the storage unit with Luke, I feel my stomach growl.

"Are you hungry, Trace?"

I laugh. "You heard that?"

"I sure did. You haven't eaten today."

"Neither have you."

"That's true." He pulls out his phone and looks at the time. "Damn, it's 5:30 already. No wonder we're both starving."

We get inside my car.

"I know just the place we can eat." I pull out of the parking lot. "Ava might want to go eat with us. Why don't you send her a text?"

"I know we're both hungry, but do you mind if we stop back at your place and get my painting first? That way we can also check in on Ava and the baby in person."

"Of course." I smile. "I'm so glad to give it to you. I wonder if you'll see more in that painting that I might have missed?"

"When I look at it again, I will let you know."

Back at Mockingbird Place, we retrieve his painting and walk over to Unit E.

Luke opens the door, and we find Ava sitting at the kitchen table studying.

"What do you have there, Luke?" she asks.

"I have a painting that I'll show you later, but right now Trace and I want to take you to Aunt Lucy's Diner for dinner. We're both starving."

She leaps to her feet. "Let me go put on some clothes. I want to get out for a while. It will be a good change of pace because my brain has quit working. Can one of you grab the diaper bag and the baby?"

"Sure thing," I answer.

"Perfect. I'll only be five minutes."

Luke places the covered painting on the sofa, and we go upstairs to get the baby. Even though the diner is only a few blocks away, we decide to take Luke's truck since we have the baby and a heavy diaper bag.

"Aunt Lucy's desserts are the best. Try to keep that in mind when you order your meal so you can leave room for something sweet," I tell them.

"Do they have pie?" Ava asks.

"They sure do. I like their chocolate cream pie. Apple is great, too. And Jackson swears the strawberry cake will blow your mind."

Luke pulls his truck out of Mockingbird Place's parking lot. "Why don't we get all three? Whatever is left over we can eat tomorrow."

"Not for me," Ava says. "I only allow myself to cheat once a week. That's the rule. I want to get my figure back as soon as I can."

Luke shakes his head. "You're so silly. Your figure looks great, sweetie."

Two minutes later, we turn the corner and see Aunt Lucy's, which looks like a building straight out of the 1940s. Its stainless steel exterior reflects the surroundings like a mirror. The inside always makes me feel like I've traveled back in time with its checkered floor, long counter, red stools, and booths lining the front window.

"You're going to love the food. Everything is delicious. And you'll love Lucy, the owner. She's sixty years old and was named after Lucille Ball. She'll tell you that she's the biggest Lucille Ball fan you'll ever meet."

We walk through the glass doors. Lucy greets us in a bright blue dress and matching high heels. "Hello, Trace. How are you today?"

"I'm great. How are you?"

"Still above the ground." She turns to Luke, Ava, and the baby. "And who do I have the pleasure of meeting today?"

Ava holds up the carrier with the baby. "This is Michael Lukas Trace Wagner."

"What a sweet baby. He looks just like his parents. Daddy's nose and mama's mouth and eyes."

"Thank you," Luke says, "But he's my nephew. His daddy and I were twins."

"*Were twins?* I'm so sorry."

"That's okay. We're just so grateful to have this wonderful boy of his in our lives." Luke introduces Ava. "I'm Luke Wagner."

"I'm Lucille Ball Morris, but everyone calls me Aunt Lucy." She leads us to a booth. "Wagner? Any relation to the actor Robert Wagner? You're so good-looking, just like him."

"Thank you, ma'am. No relations to Robert Wagner," Luke tells her. "Not that I know of anyway."

"Well, I swear you sound a lot like him. Bob had a rich, deep voice like yours. Few people know that he had the very same bungalow at Universal Studios that Lucille Ball once had." She leads us to our booth and waves over a waiter. "This is Trevor, guys. He's going to take very good care of you." She turns to him. "Trevor, their dessert is on me."

After finishing our meal and waiting for our desserts, Ava says, "If you guys will excuse me, I need to change and feed our little guy. Luke, may I have the keys to the truck?"

As she walks out of the diner, a ghost from my past holds the door open for her and then comes inside.

All the blood freezes in my veins.

Though it's been ages and he's no longer a teenager, there's no mistaking Alvin, the kid on my junior high football team.

"Is something wrong, Trace?" Luke asks.

"Don't turn around, but the guy in the blue shirt next to Aunt Lucy is Alvin, the kid I told you about. I hope he doesn't see me. I'm in no mood to talk to him tonight. Being with you at the storage unit was amazing, Luke. I took steps forward, but now, I'm coming face to face with someone from my past and it feels like I'm slipping backward."

Luke reaches across the table and takes my hand. "Let's get our desserts to go."

"Yes. Please."

He motions to Trevor.

Before our waiter gets to our table, I see Alvin walking straight toward me. "Fuck. I'm not ready for this."

Alvin stands at the end of our table, his eyes locking with mine. "Trace? It is you. Do you remember me? Alvin Carter. We were in junior high together."

"Yes, I remember you, Alvin." A storm of unwanted emotions begins to swirl inside me and my heart starts pounding faster and harder. I can see my teammates' faces in the locker room again, but especially Alvin's. Did he and the others know what was going to happen to me? I feel so transparent. Exposed. As the ancient shame tries to resurface, I push it away and latch onto the anger that is welling up inside me.

"It's so good to see you." Alvin looks at Luke, who has a worried expression on his face, and then at me. "I don't want to interrupt your meal but I would like to talk to you." He hands me his business card. "Please call me. There's so much I need to talk to you about."

I place the card on the table. "Alvin, I don't mean to be rude. We don't have anything to talk about now or ever."

"But I believe we do."

"I can't, Alvin." Standing, I turn to Luke. "I'm going to walk home. I need to clear my head."

He nods. "Okay, I understand."

As I'm leaving the diner, I hear Alvin say to Luke, "I'm so sorry. I didn't mean to upset him."

I'm a wreck, a total wreck.

Ava rolls downs a window in Luke's truck. "Where are you going?"

"Back to Mockingbird Place. I need some fresh air. Luke will tell you why."

"Okay. I'll see you back home," she says in a tone of concern.

I nod and keep walking—one foot in front of the other, trying to get as far away from the man who reminds me of what happened with Coach Shultz.

What's wrong with me? When will I ever be normal again? Is normal even possible for me? My mind is spinning out of control. How can I go from having such a wonderful time with Luke at the storage unit to feeling like I'm dying inside the moment I see Alvin? For years, my doubts and fears have been my prison. Earlier with Luke, I felt like I'd finally escaped the cage. What happened to me wasn't my fault. I'm not to blame. Luke's insights of my paintings helped me to finally realize that.

So why am I running away? Why did I treat Alvin like he was a dick? I might be better than I was before meeting Luke, but it's obvious I'm still fucked up. Is it fair for me to ask him to stick around while I work through my own crap, if I ever will be able to?

I walk through the gates of Mockingbird Place and see Harvey coming out of Unit F.

"Hey, Trace. Do you mind lending me a hand?"

"I don't mind at all." It's not entirely true. I'd rather be by myself right now, but I care a great deal for this old man. "What can I help you with, Harvey?"

"S & M are having me replace one of the upper kitchen cabinets in this unit for the new renter. I just need you to hold it while I screw it into the wall."

After we finish the job, Harvey says, "Looks like you could use a beer. I've got a couple in my cooler out on the patio. What do you say?"

"I'd like that."

He smiles and walks out the door.

A text from Luke pops up on my phone. *We're back. Where are you? Having a beer with Harvey.*

How are you doing?

Better but still need some time.

Will you come over? I have some news.

What news could he have? I'm curious. But since I'm still reeling from seeing Alvin, I'm not ready to face Luke yet. *I'll try to drop by later.*

Understand you need time alone, Trace, but please come over when you're ready no matter how late it is.

I'm not sure what I should do. So I type, *TTYL.*

Harvey walks back in with two bottles and hands me one. "Cheers."

"Cheers."

We clink our beers together and each take a sip.

"Trace, why the long face? You look like you're carrying the weight of the world on your shoulders."

"It's that obvious?"

"To an old man like me who's been around since the dinosaurs it is. All you kids who live around here meant so much to Malcolm. Well, I feel the same way. If you need to talk—I'm all ears."

"I do need to talk. It's been a very strange day. Good and bad."

"I've had those kind of days before myself. What happened?"

Where to begin? "Harvey, you know I paint."

He nods. "And I know you don't show anyone your work, though like everyone in the complex, I'm dying to see it."

"And you might get your chance, especially after what happened today. I showed Luke every painting I've ever done. It was so liberating, Harvey, but then someone from my past showed up and fucked with my head." I tell him everything, holding back nothing. About the attack. About how I got started painting. And most importantly about Luke and how I want to be with him. I don't why I'm so open with Harvey. Maybe because he reminds me a little of Malcolm. And I could always talk to Malcolm. "But I can't ask Luke to be with someone like me who is still so obviously screwed up, can I?"

"You sound like someone I used to know a long time ago. He walked away from love because he was screwed up, too." Harvey downed the rest of his beer. "He was having trouble accepting the fact that he was gay. So he ended up marrying a wonderful woman and had a child. Although there were times he was very happy, he was never truly fulfilled. When he finally decided to tell the man of his dreams how much he loved him, Malcolm died."

"Oh my God, Harvey. You're that guy."

"Yes. I've never told anyone this before. Ever. Even though S & M know how close Malcolm and I were, they don't know the whole story." Harvey sighs. "I met Malcolm before I was married and we had an affair. I was so in love with him. That never changed. God, he was so handsome and sure of himself. We were in our twenties, and the world wasn't like it is today. In fact, people could go to jail for being gay. Malcolm didn't care. He was *out and proud* before people even called it that. Me? I cared. I cared too much what people thought. I broke it off with him but we stayed friends. Close friends. And I eventually met a beautiful woman who meant so much to me. We married, built a life together, and had an amazing daughter. My wife was a wonderful person, and I never told her that I was gay. I just couldn't hurt her that way. She passed away just two weeks before Malcolm died. Wanting to respect the memory of my late wife, my plan was to tell Malcolm my true feelings sometime after the New Year. He's gone, Trace. I lost my chance for complete happiness. I don't know if Malcolm knew my true feelings, but even if he did he never said so. That doesn't surprise me. He respected and cared for my wife and she felt the same for him.

"What I'm trying to tell you, Trace, is not to waste your life thinking you're not good enough or worrying you won't be able to accept your past or letting any other reason ruin your chance at true love. Just go for it. I can tell you love Luke and he loves you. That's all that matters for a happy life. The rest you can figure out along the way. Together."

Love. What a word. So powerful and full of meaning. Is that what I'm feeling for Luke? Luke is the best thing that has ever happened to me. For the first time in my life I was able to show one of my paintings and give it to someone. Not just someone. Luke. My good-looking cowboy.

Chapter 17

Taking a deep breath, I ring the doorbell of Unit E.

Luke opens the door, wraps his arms around me, and pulls me in close. "I'm so glad you're here, Trace. Knowing how upset you were I thought you might not come."

"I wasn't sure either until I talked to Harvey." I kiss Luke, realizing how much he means to me. "I'm sorry if I worried you."

"Come inside. There's so much I need to tell you."

When I walk into the apartment, I find Ava sitting in a chair and holding the baby. The painting I gave Luke is still lying on the sofa and covered.

"Hi, Trace," she says. "I'm glad to see you're looking so much better now. The walk was good for you. Luke explained to me everything you're going through. I'm so sorry."

"The walk and a talk with a very wise man did the trick to change my mood." I turn to Luke. "Have you showed Ava your painting yet?"

"No. I was waiting for you. After all, you painted it."

I like that he's concerned with how I feel about Ava seeing my work and is leaving it up to me when to uncover the piece. "I believe now is the perfect time. Drum roll, please."

Luke grins.

I remove the cover and hold the canvas so Ava can get a clear view of it.

"I had no idea you were so good." She stares at the painting. "To be honest, I thought you weren't very good because you would never show anyone your work. Boy, was I wrong. This is absolutely amazing. Thank you so much for sharing this with me. My God, you captured both of them perfectly. I'm stunned. You never met Mick but I swear that's exactly how he stood—both hands hooked in his belt loops. Did Luke tell you about that?"

"No, but I remembered one of the photos where he was standing like that. He looked so happy and content."

Her eyes well up. "It's beautiful. Thank you for sharing it with me."

I hug her. "Thank Luke, not me. He's the one who helped me realize I need to share my work. Would you like to hang it?"

"Of course I do." She holds little Mick next to the painting. "That's your daddy and Uncle Luke, sweetie. Uncle Trace painted it." She faces Luke and me. "Let's hang it right above the sofa where we can see it every time we walk in here."

Luke puts his hand on my shoulder. "Is that okay with you, Trace?"

"I think it's the perfect beginning."

After we hang the painting, the baby starts to get fussy.

"Guys, little Mick and I are tired. I've got classes in the morning. So we're going to go upstairs and go to bed."

I hug her and kiss the baby on the forehead. "Goodnight."

Luke does the same.

After Ava shuts her door, he turns to me. "You and I didn't get to eat our desserts. What do you say?"

"Start the coffee and pass the forks." I give him a quick kiss.

I sit down at the kitchen table and watch him prepare the coffee. "Sorry I walked out the way I did. Something just came over me when I saw Alvin. I wasn't myself."

"Nothing to be sorry about." He comes out of the kitchen and puts his arms around me. "I know it must have been quite the shock after all these years. But that's why I wanted to talk with you. After you left the diner, Alvin told me some things you need to hear. I don't want to be pushy but you should know. Are you up for this, sweetheart?"

Bracing myself, I say, "I'm not letting anything stop me from moving forward, honey. Never again. Tell me what Alvin said to you."

"That motherfucker molested him, too, and some of the other boys on your team."

I'm completely shocked. "What? Are you serious? I had no clue."

"Yeah. Alvin tackled you that day because he'd seen the wickedness in Shultz's eyes for you that he had experienced himself. In his thirteen-year-old mind he thought if you got hurt Shultz wouldn't be able to molest you."

The ancient memory comes into clear view, sharp and intense. I remember Alvin's hesitation to leave the field when Coach Shultz ordered everyone but me off the field.

THEY ALL RACE to the locker room, but Alvin doesn't move. Is he in trouble?

Hoping to smooth things out between him and Coach Shultz, I say, "I'm okay, Coach. Good hit, Alvin."

Alvin smiles.

Coach Shultz puts his arm around Alvin, and the smile vanishes. "Go. It's okay. We'll talk later."

Alvin looks at me in a weird way before racing to the locker room.

"ALVIN HATED that man and he wanted to save you."

As I travel back in my mind to that horrific day again, I realize everything Luke is saying about Alvin is true.

I TAKE a step to follow Alvin to the locker room, but Coach Shultz moves in front of me.

*"Not you, Trace. Not yet. You and I are going to gather up the equipment
and put it away."*

"Yes, sir."

By the time we are done, the other boys are out of the showers and dressed.

*"Take a seat, team." Coach Shultz walks over to the white board and begins
writing out the practice times for the rest of the week. "I'll see all of you on the
field in your uniforms at four o'clock tomorrow for another scrimmage. Don't be
late. Now, get out of here."*

*As Coach Shultz finishes filling out our schedule on the white board, Alvin
says to me. "Trace, want to get a Coke with me and Jimmy and some of the
other guys before heading home?"*

"Sure. Sounds fun." I feel like part of the team now.

*Coach Shultz comes up behind me. "He'll have to take you up on that offer
another time, Alvin. I can't let one of my football players leave without a shower,
and Trace hasn't had one yet."*

Alvin shakes his head. "We'll wait."

*"No, you won't," Coach Shultz says firmly. "Get out of here. I want you
rested for tomorrow's scrimmage."*

*I'm so disappointed that I have to stay. I want to go with the other boys, but
don't let on to Coach Shultz.*

"Trace, hurry,"Alvin says. "Meet us at McDonalds."

"I will. Thanks."

He and the others leave.

"LUKE, now I understand. That bastard hurt Alvin like he hurt me.
Damn. I treated Alvin like a piece of shit at the diner."

"He understands why, Trace. Alvin knew you didn't know about
him and the others. And like you, all of Shultz's victims still haven't
had any real sense of closure because the motherfucker died before
any of you had a chance to confront him."

"Damn it. I left Alvin's business card on the table and I really
need to talk to him."

"Don't worry." Luke smiles. "I've got his card. He wanted to talk
to you, too."

The coffee pot chimes.

"I forgot about our coffee and dessert." Luke walks into the kitchen.

"What time is it?"

"Ten thirty."

"Do you think Alvin will be up?"

"I'm fairly certain he will be. He was upset when he left the diner." Luke hands me a cup of coffee and a slice of pie. "Alvin hated how he made you feel. That was the last thing he wanted to do."

"May I have his card? I'm going to call him right now."

"Sure thing."

I punch in Alvin's number.

"Hello?" An image of a younger Alvin asking me to join him and the other boys at McDonald's appears in my mind.

"Alvin, this is Trace Cotton. I called because I'm sorry I was so rude to you today."

"I'm so glad you called, because I'm the one who should be sorry. I should have never interrupted your dinner. I've just been trying to find you for so long, when I saw you sitting in that booth I completely forgot my manners."

"So did I. Alvin, you were right. We need to talk, but this isn't something we can do over the phone. When can we meet?"

"I know it's late, Trace, but now that I know where you are I want to get everything out and on the table. This has haunted me all these years. Could we meet tonight?"

"Absolutely. I think this will help both of us. Aunt Lucy's stays open twenty-four hours."

"I can be back there in fifteen minutes, Trace."

Not wanting to be alone for this, I say, "I'm going to bring Luke with me if that's okay with you."

"Sure. Very nice guy, and it's clear that he cares for you a lot. See you there."

I put my phone away and look at Luke. "Will you go with me?"

"You know I will." Luke puts our slices of pie away and jots down a quick note for Ava to let her know where we're going.

When we arrive at Lucy's, a waiter greets us. "Two of you?"

"Three. Our friend will be arriving shortly," Luke says. "We'd like that booth in the corner, please."

It's away from the other customers and will give us some privacy. I'm so glad he's with me. I'm anxious to talk with Alvin. Having Luke by my side is helping to calm me down.

Moments later, Alvin enters the diner. He comes over and sits down across from me and Luke. "Trace, thank you for doing this."

"No thanks needed. This is important to me, too."

The waiter comes over and we quickly order coffee.

After he leaves, Alvin sighs. It's clear he's as nervous about this as I am. "I've been waiting for this moment for so long, now I don't know where to start."

"Me either," I admit.

Luke leans forward. "Guys, if you don't care if I butt in, I think the beginning is the only place to start."

"You're absolutely right, honey."

"Yes, you are." Alvin nods. "That bastard hurt both of us, Trace."

"What happened to you?"

Alvin recounts how Coach Shultz abused him multiple times. The motherfucker terrified him into silence, swearing to kill him and his single mother if Alvin ever told. Being thirteen at the time, he didn't know what to do.

"But it wasn't just me," Alvin says. "Jim, Kyle, and Eddie also. Poor Daniel, too. He committed suicide two years ago."

"I remember Daniel." My hate for Coach Shultz multiplies.

"But you were the last the bastard abused before he died. I'm so sorry, Trace. I wanted to save you that day. I tried. I really tried."

"Alvin, I never blamed you. You were just a kid like me." Seeing the tears in his eyes moves me. "Please don't think that what happened to me was in any way your fault."

"It's just so hard. After you didn't come back to school I was so close to telling, but I was scared for my mother's safety. And then the motherfucker died. I was so glad he was gone, but the nightmares continued. It took a lot of therapy before I could sleep through the night. Still, every month or so to this day, I wake up screaming after seeing Coach Shultz's twisted grin in my sleep."

"You never got closure, Alvin," Luke says. "It's the same for Trace. There must be some way to help you and the other guys."

"I wish there were, but I don't think there is. I've tried to find closure. I want to put this behind me. I've even been back to our old school, Trace. I thought if I could walk those halls, see the locker room, the showers—something would click inside me that would finally put the whole thing to rest. But it didn't work. Actually, it made things worse for a while." Alvin's hands curl into fists. "They have a fucking memorial wall with the bastard's photo next to the trophy cases. Can you believe that?"

"Actually, I can. When he died, the school went into mourning. I saw it on the news with my parents. All the teachers and students turned Shultz into a saint after his heart attack and collision with the tree. After that it was too late for closure."

"Yeah," Alvin says. "When I saw that fucking memorial wall I wanted to rip everything off it and tear them to shreds."

"That's it." Luke grabs my hand. "That's the closure you need, sweetheart—you, Alvin and the other guys. We need to have a demolition party and rip that memorial wall apart."

"You're serious?"

He smiles. "I am."

"But is that even possible?" Alvin asks. "It's school property. We would go to jail if we marched in there and tore the place up. Principal Harris is still there, but she doesn't have a clue about Coach Shultz. Even if we all told her what happened, I doubt she would go along with it after all these years."

"Alvin, just leave it to me. I'm not just a cowboy. I can work magic. I've got an idea. Let me handle this. Can you contact the other guys about this?"

"I can." Alvin smiles, clearly getting excited about the possibility of some kind of closure Luke is suggesting.

Even though I have no clue as to how Luke is going to make this happen, I know he will.

We continue talking—not just about Shultz, but also about our lives now. Alvin is engaged to a nurse named Cheryl who works at Parkland. He's working on his business degree online and plans on getting his master's degree at my university after he graduates.

"And what about you two?" he asks. "How long have you been together?"

Luke smiles and looks at his watch.

Chapter 18

After saying good-bye to Alvin in the diner's parking lot, Luke and I walk over to the truck. Before he starts the engine, I reach over and put my hand on his leg. It feels so natural, like we've been together forever. Does he feel the same way? I hope so.

As he pulls out of the parking lot, I say, "I thought you were cute when you looked at the time on your phone to answer Alvin's question."

"Cute? Me? You're the cute one. And what question are you talking about?"

"When he asked us how long we'd been together. And yes, you're cute. Handsome. Adorable."

"You're definitely good for my ego, Trace," he says. "It hasn't been very long since we first laid eyes on each other, sweetheart, and even a shorter time since we started going out. And besides, we haven't made it official. But I'd like to."

"You mean you want us to be *exclusive*?"

"That's exactly what I want."

I lean my head on his shoulder. "I want that too."

Luke suddenly pulls the truck over to the side of the road.

I sit up straight. "Did we have a flat?"

"No, you gorgeous guy. We're official now. This needs to be sealed with a kiss." He pulls me in close, stares at me with his big brown eyes, and gently caresses my lips with his. "Trace, I want you to spend the night with me."

"Yes, that's where I want to be."

When we walk inside Unit E, we find the lights are off. Only the tiny night-lights that Ava put in throughout the apartment illuminate our way. She doesn't want anyone tripping in the dark if they are carrying little Mick for his early morning feedings.

Luke grabs the baby monitor receiver off the coffee table. The sounds coming from the speaker let us know that both momma and baby are fast asleep.

He and I tiptoe quietly up the stairs, not wanting to wake them. Before we reach the landing, I trip on the last step. Luke catches me before I go tumbling down, but I end up on my back. We both start laughing.

"Shh, Luke."

He nods. But the more we try to be quiet the louder we get.

"Stop. We have to stop." I'm sprawled out on the floor.

Luke reaches down to try to help me up, but I'm so weak from laughing I end up pulling him down on top of me instead, which only sends us into another fit of laughter.

As we try to scramble to our feet, Ava opens her door.

"What on earth is going on, you two?" When her eyes land on us, she grins. "I can see what's happening, but wouldn't Luke's bedroom be more comfortable than the landing's hard floor? You're lucky you didn't wake the baby. I just changed and fed him. He just got to sleep. I would suggest you use the bedroom for your shenanigans so the rest of us can get some sleep."

"Shenanigans?" I smile. "That's a word you don't hear very often."

"She picked it up from my mother, Trace. Mom's half Irish."

"Actually, it's the nicest word I could think of." With her hands on her hips and a smile on her face she says, "Go to your room. Goodnight, guys."

When she closes the door, we rush into Luke's bedroom because we are still laughing.

As he places the baby monitor on the nightstand, I try to calm down but that only makes it worse. "I can't...*ha ha*...figure out...*ha ha*...how to stop...*ha ha*...laughing...Luke."

Through his chuckles, Luke says, "I have so much fun with you, Trace, no matter what we're doing."

Starting to gain my composure, I sit down on the edge of the bed. "That's nice of you to say, and I feel the same way about you."

He moves next to me and wraps his arms around my shoulders, pressing his lips to mine. The hysterics vanish completely, replaced by an uncontrollable desire for him. "I want you, sweetheart. I want to be inside you."

I sigh, feeling concern wash over me. "We haven't had *that* discussion, have we? Top? Bottom? Versatile? I guess we need to if we're taking this to the next level."

"I guess we do. So? Which are you, sweetheart?"

"I've always been a top, Luke. What about you?" I hold my breath, waiting for his answer.

"Me, too."

I feel like my insides are about to rip apart. "Damn."

He smiles. "Not damn, baby. Not damn at all. I have a pretty good idea why you always top."

"I know you do. You know everything there is to know about me, Luke. The one time I tried to bottom for a guy it didn't go well. The memory came back and I almost punched him. Thankfully, I came to my senses and ended things before it got messy."

Luke brushes his lips against my neck. "Trace, I may have always topped before but that just means I haven't been with the right guy to be on the receiving end...until now." He kisses me deeply, tangling his tongue with mine.

I can't believe what I'm hearing. He's willing to try because of me. I feel warm all over. This is where I belong. With Luke. Arms entwined together, lips to lips, body to body. "Are you sure?"

"Yes, I'm sure, sweetheart. A little anxious, but ready." He opens his nightstand drawer, and pulls out some condom packages, a clean towel, and a new bottle of lube. He places them on the mattress next to us. "I went to the Condoms Sense store on Cedar Springs earlier. As you can see, I was hoping tonight might end up with you in my bed."

I grin. "I can see that."

Luke removes my shirt, tossing it to the side.

The breeze from his ceiling fan hits my flesh. A hot shiver rolls through my body.

I can't stop staring at his brown eyes.

"God, you're so damn hot, Trace." His tone is filled with lust, which is turning me on more and more.

I unbutton his shirt and pull it off of him. I run my hands up and down his muscled torso. My heart races faster and faster. Immense desire for him quakes through my entire being. Since the first day I met Luke, I've been mesmerized by him. Totally enthralled. It's even more powerful now. I can't resist him, not that I want to.

Sucking on his neck, I pinch his nipples lightly and then I hear a passionate moan from him.

I kiss him again, removing his belt with one hand and cupping the back of his neck with the other. I pull the leather strap until it is free of the loops and toss it to the floor. My hunger for him is growing in intensity. I need him. I need to be inside him. Continuing to devour his mouth, I unzip him. I squeeze his cock through the fabric of his underwear. I capture his groans in my mouth. He's hard. Hard for me.

I kiss my way down his gorgeous body and remove his jeans and black briefs. Wrapping my hand around his cock, I stroke him several times while cupping his balls. I lick the tip of his cock, drinking in his first salty drop.

More wonderful moans escape his lips.

"Roll over, honey," I tell him.

Once he's face down, I part his beautiful ass cheeks and begin licking him.

"Oh my God, Trace. Damn. So good. You're driving me wild."

His words get me going. I'm so freaking hot and my cock is so damn hard. Continuing to bathe his ass, I reach between his legs and wrap my hand around him, giving him a nice squeeze.

Luke moans again. "Ahh. Yes. Good. Fucking good."

Insane with lust for him, I strip out of the rest of my clothes, put on a condom, and squirt some lube into the palm of my hand. Slickening up his backside, I feel him stiffen for a moment when I circle his tight ring with my index finger.

"Just relax, honey. We're going to take this nice and slow."

He lets out a long, hot breath. "I'm okay. I want this. I want you."

I finger his anus and slowly pierce him.

"Ohh."

I pull my finger out. "You okay?"

"I'm fine. Don't stop, baby. Please, don't stop." He writhes on the bed, fisting his sheets.

Continuing to stroke his cock, I push my finger deeper into Luke. In and out. Over and over. I add another finger. The more he wiggles on the bed the hotter I get.

I crawl on top of him, positioning the head of my cock at his entrance. "If you need me to stop or pull out or whatever, just say so."

"For crying out loud, Trace, fuck me already. I'm dying to have you inside me." Every manic word that slips from his lips is filled with heat and passion.

As much as I want to throw caution to the wind and slam into his hot body, I will myself to inch into him slowly.

He shifts back slightly, taking more of me. "Okay. Okay. I'm okay."

Kissing the back of his neck, I realize his words are for him as much as for me.

Another inch.

"Yes, Trace. Yes."

Another.

"Hell. Oh. Wait. Okay. Okay. I'm ready for more."

Methodically, I continue moving deeper into his body, with my breaths coming out in fiery bursts until finally I'm all the way in. "You okay, honey?"

With his head to the side and eyes closed, Luke is clinging to his pillow with both hands. "Yep, just don't move yet."

"I won't. Breathe. Nice and slow."

His breaths first come out ragged but eventually steady. I remain frozen in place, waiting for him to give me a signal as to whether to continue making love to him or to pull out. This must be what it feels like to a racecar whose driver has one foot on the gas and one on the break, if racecars could feel. My engine's rpms are definitely in the red zone but as hard as it is to stay put I must. For Luke. His needs are all that matter to me.

"Damn. I never imagined…damn. Trace, this is fucking unbelievable. Wow." He shoves his ass back and forth, sliding up and down me.

That's all it takes. He's given me the green flag. Time to let off the brake and head around the track. I begin pumping into him. In and out. Over and over. Each thrust is fueled with more passion than I've ever felt before.

"I want to get on my back, sweetheart. I need to see your face."

I pull out of his body and he flips around.

Now that I can see his handsome face, my lust goes into overdrive. I grab his ankles, spreading his legs wide. I shift forward and he grabs my cock, helping to guide it back into his ass.

Completely lost in this incredible moment with him, I thrust into him again and again.

"Yes, Trace. Yes." Luke wraps his hands around my neck and stares at me with those big brown eyes. "More. Please. Don't stop. God. Whatever you do, don't stop."

"I won't, honey. I promise. I won't until you come for me."

With one hand remaining around my neck, he shoves the other between his legs and begins wildly fisting himself. "So close. So close, Trace."

"So am I, honey. So am I."

After a few more powerful thrusts, I feel his insides tighten on my cock like a vise.

"Coming. Fuuck."

Seeing his cream land on his face, chest, and stomach sends me over the edge. My entire body stiffens as every ounce of energy I have is funneled to this single moment of absolute connection. As I climax I can feel my cock pulsing inside him.

Pulling out, I collapse on top of him, feeling his cream on my skin. Even though it's hard to catch my breath, I kiss him. And he kisses me back.

I've never had sex that meant this much to me before. "That was incredible, honey. Mind blowing."

"Mind and body." He smiles. "This makes it official, sweetheart. We are definitely exclusive. You're mine. I'm not sharing you with anyone."

"You don't have to worry about that, you sexy beast. You've ruined me for other men."

"That's music to my ears."

We hear little Mick start to fuss on the baby monitor.

"I got it," we say in unison and start laughing again.

"Let's both go," he says, pulling on his jeans. "Ava needs her sleep."

"I'll get the baby, you warm his bottle."

"Deal."

Quietly, I enter Ava's bedroom. Yawning, she's just finishing changing the baby.

"Give him to me, sweetie. You go back to sleep."

She nods, hands me the baby, and climbs back into her bed.

I head downstairs with little Mick, passing the photos of his mom and dad's wedding. "How's my big boy doing?"

His eyes are wide open and staring at me.

"Want to know a secret? I think I'm falling in love with Uncle Luke, but don't tell anyone, okay. That will be our secret."

I sit down in the chair where all three of us like to feed the baby. It's the most comfy for the job because of the armrests.

Luke comes out of the kitchen with little Mick's bottle. He leans over and kisses him on the forehead, hands me the bottle, and then kisses me.

After we finish feeding the baby, we put him to bed. Thankfully, Ava doesn't stir from her sleep.

Luke and I take a shower together, enjoying each other's body once again. After we're done, we go back to Luke's bedroom and fall asleep in each other's arms.

JUST BEFORE SIX o'clock I wake up and crawl out of Luke's bed.

"Where you going?" he asks sleepily.

I lean down and kiss him. "To my apartment, honey. I want to get some fresh clothes. Go back to sleep. Come over when you wake up."

"Okay, sweetheart. Love you."

Those last two words hit me like a thunderbolt, but before I can take a breath, I can tell he's fallen back to sleep. Did he realize what he said to me? No. He couldn't have. God, what I would give if he meant it. But it's too soon for those words. Way too soon.

Or is it?

Chapter 19

As Ava and Jackson leave for class, Luke walks in talking on the phone and carrying the baby.

I hold out my arms, and he hands little Mick to me.

"That's right," Luke says into his phone.

I gaze into the baby's eyes. God, he is so beautiful. "Good morning, my little precious cowboy. I just love you to the moon and back. Yes I do. Always will. Uh huh."

He curls his tiny hand around my finger, warming my heart.

Luke smiles, continuing his call. "It's all set, Alvin. Six o'clock tonight. We'll see you and the other guys there."

When he puts away his phone, I ask, "It's on? You were able to make it happen?"

He puts his arm around my shoulder. "Yes, sweetheart. It's on. Could I have a cup of coffee while I tell you how I worked my magic?"

"Make yourself at home. I just made a fresh pot. We also have bagels and cream cheese. Now will you please tell me?"

"I just went down and talked to the superintendent. You have heard of Dr. Wagner, haven't you?"

I grin. "Don't tell me you're related to him."

He laughs. "You mean Uncle James? I sure am related to him."

"That's too good to be true."

"Maybe so but it *is* true. He's my dad's older brother. Anyway, I just told Uncle James everything. I got a call from Principal Harris early this morning. The rest you know. She and Uncle James are going to meet us and the other guys at the school tonight for our demolition party."

"You did it, Luke. I can't believe this. Thank you so much." I lean over and kiss him as a rush of emotions roll through me. "I'm actually excited, though a bit apprehensive, too."

"Of course you are, sweetheart. But I truly believe this is going to be the closure you need."

"I think you're right. For me and Alvin and the rest of the guys." I look at little Mick, who's fallen asleep in my arms. "I'm ready to let go of the past, Luke, and start moving into the future. It's brighter than ever before."

We put the baby in the crib that Jackson bought for this apartment. Jackson wanted to make sure that he had everything necessary to babysit little Mick and even keep him overnight. He's nuts about the baby just like everyone else in the complex, including Tony. That was a big surprise to me, especially him being such a tough, brooding MMA fighter. But whenever Tony is around our baby, he becomes a total marshmallow when he thinks no one else is looking.

"Now what?" I ask, looking at my phone. "How are we going to pass the time until six o'clock?"

"After I eat this delicious bagel, I thought this would be a good time for a long walk and a visit with each one of our neighbors who are at home. Everybody in the complex has asked me to bring the baby to their apartments."

"He's going to be so spoiled." I smile. "Little Mick is all anyone can talk about around here. Can you imagine how it's going to be when Lashaya and Hayden have their baby? Mockingbird Place's residents are going to lose their minds with joy."

"Very true but maybe the spoiling won't be so bad when he has to share the attention with the new baby."

"Don't count on it."

When we knock on Unit C's door, Eli comes out and his eyes light up the instant he sees the baby. "How's my little fireman? I've got a present for him, guys. I know he's too small now but we have to be prepared. Come on inside." With a big smile on his face, Eli hands a toy fire truck to Luke.

The same thing happens when Jaris opens his door. Doc gives little Mick a onesie with the words "Dr. Mick" on the front and "Future MD" on the back.

This adoration is repeated at every stop.

Since Luke is carrying all of Mick's gifts, I push the baby's stroller as we make our way to S & M's place. They saw us just before we went into Tony's apartment and offered to make us lunch.

"Trace, this feels like Christmas. All these presents. Ava is going to flip."

"I bet she is. Where in the world did Tony find those baby boxing gloves? They are so cute."

"And what about the tiny robe he bought the baby that says 'Little Champ' on the back?" Luke grins. "Tony is just a big old teddy bear even if he doesn't want any of us to know it."

"Definitely." I ring the doorbell.

Sarah rushes out and leans down, looking at the baby. "Oh my goodness. He's getting even more adorable every day."

"And what about us, Sarah?" Luke chuckles. "Are we more adorable than the last time you saw us?"

She hugs us. "Of course you are. Come inside. Lunch is about ready. I want you to meet our new neighbor who is moving into Unit F."

We walk into her apartment. Martha is at the table with a young, handsome priest.

"Guys, this is Father Stephen Norelli," Sarah says. "Father, this is Luke Wagner and Trace Cotton. But the most important person in the room is this angel, Michael Lukas Trace Wagner."

The priest and Martha jump up and surround the stroller.

"Nice to meet you guys. And your baby is beautiful."

I realize that Father Stephen is a very intelligent man.

"Thank you, Father," Luke says. "We think so too."

"Won't you join us for lunch, Stephen?" Sarah asks.

"I would love to but I really need to be going," he says. "I'll start moving in the first."

"If you need any help, I live in Unit D," I tell him. "And I'm sure your other neighbors will be happy to help too."

"I might take you up on that offer, Trace. Thanks." He says good-bye to us and then leaves.

"Nice guy," Luke says.

Martha nods. "He was just ordained and took a job at St. Paul's Episcopal Church as their associate rector."

Little Mick wakes up.

"Come to Aunt Martha, angel." She lifts him out of the stroller. "S, can you get lunch on the table while I take care of the baby?"

"Of course, honey. Just as long as I get a chance to hug on him too."

We enjoy a wonderful lunch with S & M, and they too have more presents for the baby.

On the way back to Luke's place, he turns to me. "At this rate, we're going to have to build another floor onto Unit E just to hold Mick's presents."

"We just might and I'm sure S & M and Oliver would approve the construction." Why did I say we? Because I'm already picturing myself living with Luke. Even though it's only been a short time since we've gotten to know each other, I can't imagine not being with him. Hell, we haven't even said those three little words and I'm already moving in.

The rest of the afternoon slips by quickly. Ava and Jackson return from their classes around two, and Luke and I take a drive together out to the ranch he'll be working at.

He introduces me to the foreman and then asks if we could saddle up two horses.

"Take Molly and Old Gray. They need the exercise. Take them

up to the north pasture. There's a hill near there with a terrific view. On clear days you can see downtown Dallas."

Luke leads me to the barn.

"You never cease to surprise me, cowboy." I smile. "I never expected I'd be going horseback riding with you today."

"It's one of the greatest ways to get rid of stress."

"Maybe for you, but I'm stressing because I don't know how to ride."

"Don't worry. I'll be next to you the entire time."

He won't take no for an answer and it turns out I am a natural. This is a blast.

When we get the horses back in their stalls, I say, "Can we do this again, honey?"

"You betcha. What happened to your stress?"

"All gone. Right now I feel like I could destroy an entire building with my bare hands." I look at the time. "Let's go meet Alvin and the other guys for our demolition party."

When he pulls his truck into one of the parking spots at the school, a wave of anticipation rolls through me. Is Luke right? Will tearing down the bastard's memorial wall give us the closure we've needed?

The other four guys are already waiting for us by the door, and so are Superintendent Wagner and Principal Harris.

Seeing my old teammates thrills me. Even though I haven't been around them in years, I feel a bond with them because of our shared tragedy. I shake their hands, immediately recognizing each one of them—Jim, Kyle, and Eddie. And then an image of Daniel pops up in my mind. I wish he was here with us.

Alvin turns to Principal Harris and Luke's uncle. "You can't imagine how much this means to us."

I nod. "Thank you for making this happen."

Principal Harris sighs. "I just wish I had known, Trace. Guys, this is Superintendent Wagner."

We shake his hand.

"Shall we, gentlemen?" Luke's uncle holds the door open for us.

Walking into my old school is so surreal. None of us say a word. It feels so somber.

The trophy cases full of the awards the school has won in sports, music, and academics are lined against the wall opposite the entrance. On the wall to the side of the case with the sports accolades is a poster-sized framed picture of the bastard who has been the center of my nightmares since I was twelve years old. There are also framed newspaper articles, more photos, and other items praising Coach Shultz and listing his accomplishments in the community as if he were a saint. It sickens me.

I look at the others, who are just as fixed on the image of our predator as I am.

The color in Jim's face drains away, and he turns around, racing for the door. "Sorry, guys. I need a second."

I run after him and realize so are Alvin, Kyle, and Eddie.

Jim is bent over with his hands on his knees, gagging. We surround him. I see Luke's uncle and Principal Harris standing on the steps. Where's Luke?

I put my hand on Jim's back. "Just breathe nice and slow."

Luke runs out of the school bare-chested with his T-shirt in his hands. "Take this, Trace. I wetted it down at the drinking fountain."

I rub Jim's face and neck with Luke's soaked T-shirt. Luke steps back, giving the five of us space, though he doesn't go as far as the steps where his uncle and Principal Harris are still standing. It's clear to me he wants to be close enough if we need him. *If I need him.*

"Should we call 9-1-1?" Principal Harris yells over to us.

"No. I'm...fine," Jim chokes out. As he starts to recover, his color returns to his cheeks. "When I saw his face on the wall I thought I was going to pass out. I didn't know it was going to hit me like that. I'm so sorry, guys."

"Don't be sorry, Jim," Eddie says. "Looking at the fucker's face made me sick to my stomach."

"Same here." Kyle puts his arm around Jim.

I nod, realizing how much these guys mean to me. "It was like getting the wind knocked out of me."

"You okay now, Jim?" Alvin asks.

He straightens up, determination appearing on his face. "Yes. Let's do this."

We march back inside like a military unit heading to the battlefield.

Standing once again at the memorial to the monster, Alvin says, "How do we do this?"

Eddie removes one of the newspaper articles and places it on the floor. "Like this, I guess. One thing at a time. Who wants to go next?"

Jim steps up and takes down a letter from a former mayor of Dallas. "Lies. All lies." He folds it in half and sets it on top of the pile Eddie has started.

Next, Kyle removes Shultz's college diploma. "Asshole. Sorry, Principal Harris."

She wipes tears from her eyes. "Nothing to be sorry about, Kyle."

Following the other guy's examples, Alvin takes down another newspaper article and adds it to the pile—a pile of shame. "Your turn, Trace."

I stare into the eyes of the beast who nearly ruined my entire life. If it hadn't been for my loving parents, my counselor, my paintings, and now Luke, I'm not sure I would have made it to this day. Why had the other guys chosen newspaper articles and letters to remove from the wall but no photos? Is it because even though the motherfucker is dead he still has some kind of hold on us? I feel my pulse thrumming in my veins as my eyes move away from the large photo of Shultz to another letter of praise. Are we still afraid of him in some strange way? Am I?

I force my gaze back to the portrait, staring directly into his wicked eyes. "The children who now attend this school have no clue this is the image of a predator smiling at them every day when they walk by. Why are we leaving this portrait of Shultz still hanging?" I feel my hands trembling as I remove the photo from the wall. I carefully place it on top of the pile. "Is this the closure we want? I'm glad we're doing this but it doesn't feel like I hoped it would. Something is not right."

Luke puts his arm around me. "I can tell you what's not right, Trace. You guys are still feeling the fear. You're not boys any more. You're grown men now. It's time to dig deep and let your anger out. Rip this shit to shreds."

His words are like light blazing in the darkness. I can see the impact on the other guys' faces. They feel it too.

I pick up the portrait. "I'm not afraid of you anymore. You can't hurt me. Fuck you. Fuck you. Fuck you." I smash its frame on the ground, shattering the glass. Filled with rage, I remove the large picture from the ruined frame and tear it in half. I hand it to Alvin.

"Take this, you motherfucker." He pokes his fingers through the bastard's eyes.

Jim is next, and rips off the top of Shultz's head, scalping him. "Now who is the worthless piece of shit?"

Eddie and Kyle take their turns, and with each tear I feel lighter —the ancient weight lifting.

In a righteous frenzy, we destroy everything that had hung on the wall, filling the floor with debris. When there is nothing left for us to demolish, we stare at the remains of Coach Shultz.

"Now what?" Eddie asks.

"Now it's time to take out the trash once and for all." Luke hands each of us a broom and dustpan. Being so intent in our demolition party, we weren't aware he'd left to get them.

Superintendent Wagner walks over to us with a large black garbage can. "Gentlemen."

We sweep the rubbish into our dustpans and toss the fucker's remains into the can.

Once the floor is completely clean, Principal Harris says, "Boys, get that bastard out of my school."

We cheer, yell, and hug each other. Together we run out the door and empty the scum into the dumpster.

Tears of relief are streaming down our faces.

I look at my friends. "Guys, how about a moment of silence for Daniel?"

They all nod and we close our eyes, remembering our friend. I realize how lucky we are.

After a few minutes, Jim breaks the silence. "Oh my God, this feels amazing."

Alvin nods. "We're completely free."

"At last." Eddie smiles and wipes his eyes.

"I never dreamed this would happen," Kyle says.

"It happened, guys," I say. "This is closure."

Chapter 20

I nside Joey's Sports Bar & Grill, I look around the table and see the changes on everyone's faces. Luke sits on one side of me and Alvin sits on the other side. Eddie, Kyle, and Jim are across from us. Principal Harris and Superintendent Wagner are sitting on each end of the table.

"Let me kick off this celebration," the superintendent says. "The first round is on me, gentlemen."

Once we have our drinks, Alvin stands. "A toast. First, to Principal Harris and Superintendent Wagner. Thank you for allowing us to tear up your school."

Everyone laughs.

I'm so happy and full of joy. It feels so good to laugh together.

"Seriously," Alvin continues. "Thank you both. We'll never forget what you did for us tonight."

We clink our glasses together and take a drink.

Alvin turns to Luke. "But most of all I want to offer up a toast to you, Luke. You made tonight happen. You realized what the five of us needed when we couldn't see it for ourselves. This was your idea. You called your uncle and got the ball rolling. And then when we were still struggling with our emotions taking down that bastard's memorial wall, you told us to dig deep and connect with our anger. You helped us let go of all the rage inside us. And to top it all off, you handed us the brooms to sweep up Shultz's shit. I can't explain how it felt when the five of us emptied the garbage into the dumpster except to say that horrible part of my life is finally over. You gave us closure. To Luke."

"To Luke," we all say in unison.

Filled with pride for Luke, I grab his hand.

During another round of drinks and some appetizers, we get reacquainted with each other and decide that we're going to make this a monthly event.

"So you guys just met recently?" Jim asks Luke and me.

"That's right," we say in unison.

"Huh. You seem like you've been together for years to me."

"Yes it does," Eddie says.

Kyle nods. "The way they look at each other is one clue you can't miss."

Luke's uncle says with a big grin. "I think Mick would be very happy for you, Luke. Trace is a terrific guy."

"I think so too."

"Have your parents met him yet?"

He smiles. "Not yet."

I laugh. "Guys, we just started dating each other. First things first. There's no rush."

"Oh there isn't?" Luke kisses me on the cheek and then grins. "We might need to have a talk about that later, sweetheart."

Jim turns to the others. "See what I mean about these two?"

Everyone at the table seems to agree with him.

Luke's uncle not only picks up the first round, he pays for our entire bill.

We say good-bye to each other and Luke and I walk to his truck.

Before he can turn the key, I wrap my arms around his neck and kiss him. "I just can't explain... It's...overwhelming. I'm...overwhelmed. You saved me. There are just...no words...to tell you how I feel. Well, maybe there are." I kiss him again. "I love you. I love you. I love you, Luke Wagner, with all my heart."

"You say I saved you. Well, you saved me too. After my brother died I was lost. There was no joy left in my life. Everything was gray and empty. But then I met you, my beautiful man." He presses his lips to mine. "I love you, Trace Cotton. I've never loved anyone as much as you. You're the man of my dreams."

We hear whistling and cheering. We look out the windows and see Alvin, Jim, Eddie, and Kyle clapping their hands and shouting, "Happiness forever."

"I was right," Jim yells. "They belong together."

As Luke and I drive away, we lower our windows and yell back to them. "Happiness forever."

"See you next month," Alvin calls out.

As Luke turns the truck onto Lemmon Avenue, I say, "I'd like to take a detour before we head back to Mockingbird Place."

"Where to?"

"My storage unit so we can grab several of my paintings to take back with us. I want to show them to Ava and Jackson."

"I'm so proud of you, Trace."

As we begin gathering up some of the boxes containing my pieces, I send a group text to Ava and Jackson. *Have some things I want to show you. Can we meet at Luke and Ava's place in twenty minutes?*

I'll be there, Jackson texts back. *Should I bring a bottle of wine?*

Yes, please.

Ava's text comes next. *Little Mick and I will be waiting for you.*

I put my phone away.

"Are you nervous about this?" Luke asks me.

"Not at all. I'm excited. How many are in your truck now?"

"Nine. This one will make ten."

"That's enough this time." I want Ava and Jackson to see all my pieces. In fact, I want all my friends at Mocking Place to see my paintings. No more hiding them away.

Carrying a few boxes, we walk into Unit E.

Ava is sitting in a chair holding the baby, and Jackson is staring at the painting of Luke on the horse with Mick standing in the background.

"Oh my God, Trace," Jackson says. "This is gorgeous. Wow. I

LEE SWIFT

can't stop looking at it. I'm so proud of you for having the courage to show this to us."

"If you're proud of me for my courage now, then you're going to go nuts when I show you the rest of these." I laugh and lean the boxes I'm carrying against the side of the sofa.

"Are you serious? What's come over you?"

"Pour the wine while Luke and I go get the rest of the paintings and then I'll tell you."

Jackson's eyes widen. "There's more?"

"Yes. A lot," Luke says. "There's still more we couldn't bring."

Jackson smiles. "Would you believe I've never got to see his paintings before?"

"Yes, I can believe that." Luke puts his arm around me. "You're going to love them. We'll be right back."

As we unload the boxes into the apartment, Ava takes the baby upstairs and places him in his crib. It doesn't take too long and when we bring in the last load, Ava and Jackson have put together a tray of cheese and opened a bottle of wine.

After they hand Luke and me our glasses, Jackson turns to me. "Why the sudden change of heart about showing your work, Trace?"

"It's a long story."

"Let's sit," Ava says, moving to the big chair.

Jackson sits down in the chair next to her.

After Luke and I take our seats on the sofa, we tell them everything that happened today.

Jackson puts down his glass, leaves his chair, and hugs me. "Trace, I'm so happy for you. I've seen you struggle with this for years. My God, you even look different."

"Yes, you do." Ava reaches over and takes my hand. "I can see it in your eyes. All that sadness is completely gone."

"It sure is," I say. "And I wanted you two to be the first I unveil my paintings for, although I plan on sharing them with everyone."

"Let's get this party going then." Jackson rubs his hands together. It's very clear he's excited. "Don't you think I've waited long enough to see these?"

"Yes you have." I pick up the first box. "Keep in mind, you two, I'm not sure what is inside these. I've never labeled the boxes before."

"Less talking and more showing," Jackson orders with a smile. "But I think it would be wise if you labeled them when you put them back in their boxes."

I grin and turn to Luke and Ava. "Have you met my roommate, Mr. OCD?"

"Some call it a disease," he says. "I call it being organized."

Ava jumps to her feet. "I've got a black marker."

She and Jackson's words of praise after seeing the first three paintings give me such joy.

"Let's see what's inside box number four." I pull out the canvas and immediately Jackson's eyes light up.

"You painted me, Trace. I'm overwhelmed."

Ava moves closer. "It's incredible."

The image on the canvas is of Jackson in Mockingbird Place's pool.

"That water looks so real," he says, smiling. "This is freaking sick. Totally fantastic. And me? It's like a photograph, only better. Trace, you made me look hot. I like the tan you gave me."

We all laugh.

"When in the hell did you do this? I never posed for you."

"I don't know how to explain it. It's just in my head. I can see you. That's how it always works for me."

"Whatever you do, just keep doing it, Trace," Ava says. "You're an unbelievable talent."

"You know you could have made a bundle on these." Jackson hugs me. "And now this one belongs to me. I now own a Trace Cotton original."

"Yes, you do, buddy. It's worth at least three dollars and fifty cents."

"More than that, I'm sure. For me it's priceless, and I bet serious art collectors would pay dear for it and your other works too." Jackson grabs his painting. "I better go. I still have class tomorrow."

"I'll see you in the morning," Ava says.

"Goodnight." Jackson leaves.

LUKE REFILLS MY WINE GLASS. "AVA?"

"No more for me. One glass is my limit. I'm still nursing. Besides, you heard Jackson. I have class in the morning, too. Goodnight, guys."

I hug her. "Goodnight."

Luke kisses her on the forehead. "Night, sweetie."

When we hear Ava close her bedroom door, Luke turns to me. "What Jackson said about your paintings gives me an idea."

I take a sip of my wine. "I love your ideas, honey. What is it?"

"It's a surprise."

"It is?"

"Yep." He kisses me. "And I think you'll love it. Just a few things to work out first."

"I love you, Luke."

Another warm kiss. "I love you, too."

What Luke doesn't know is I have an idea of my own to surprise him, but mine has to do with sex. I trust him. I know I can do this with him. More than that even. I want to do this with him. He won't have to wait long. Once we go up to his bedroom, he'll find out what I have in store for him.

Alone in Luke's bedroom, I scan the space again. This is where we became exclusive and made love.

"What are you looking at, sweetheart?"

"A chest of drawers. A bed. A nightstand. A lamp. Your big rodeo belt buckles displayed on the shelves."

He grins. "You've been in here before."

"Yes, but I didn't realize how special this place is. I want to memorize every detail."

He holds me close. "You'll have plenty of time for that. This is your home now. This is our place. I didn't realize how much Mockingbird Place would mean to me, but with you next to me it means everything. Always."

"Always."

"And forever."

I feel the tears in my eyes, tears of joy. This amazing man found a way to give me the closure I needed so desperately. The memory of Coach Shultz might still come forward from time to time, but now I have the power to push him away. *Because of my wonderful cowboy.*

"Trace, I need you spending every night here from now on."

"You want me to move in? Shouldn't you discuss that with Ava first? And I definitely need to talk to Jackson."

"Already have—with both of them."

"When did you have a chance to do that? I've been next to you almost every moment for the past few days."

He nods. "Almost every moment, but not every one of them. I found the time." He slides his hands down my sides and captures my gaze with his sexy eyes. "Mom and Dad are coming on Sunday. It works out great since Monday is a university holiday. Ava won't have any classes. They want to spend time with her and the baby. I've told them all about you. They can't wait to meet you and I can't wait for you to meet them. I'd like you to be all settled in before they arrive."

"Wow. We're already at the meeting-the-parents stage. I can't wait for you to meet my parents either. They'll love you. They're visiting my mother's sister in Canada until next week, but as soon as they get back I'm going to have them over to meet you."

"I love that idea. I'm looking forward to meeting them. So what do you say, Trace? Want to live here with me?"

"I definitely do want to move in, but I still need to talk with Jackson myself."

"He said that you would say that." Luke smiles. "Of course, sweetheart. Talk to him. I know how close you two are. Just as long as you end up living here."

"My God, what you've done for me. It's overwhelming. And not just for me but for Alvin and the others. Without you making it happen I would still be under that dark cloud. But no more. I'm free." I wrap my arms around him. "I love you."

"And I love you." He kisses me. "Forever."

"Forever. Now, sexy, ready for my surprise?"

"Of course. Show me."

I don't waste any time and pull him in closer, pressing my lips to his. My heart is racing. I start kissing Luke's neck.

Whispering against his skin, I say, "You mean the world to me. God, I would do anything for you."

"And you mean the world to me, sweetheart. That feels so good. I'm so damn hot for you."

"You like this?" Continuing to suck on his neck, I pinch his nipples through his shirt.

"Oh yeah, baby."

"And this?" I reach down and cup his cock and balls through his jeans. Touching his hard-on pleases me. I like that I'm having such an impact on him. It makes me feel powerful and in charge.

"Hell yeah."

I remove his shirt and start sucking on his nipples. "What about this?"

"You're driving me wild, baby." His hands tug at my hair. "Feels great."

Getting down on my knees, I take off his pants and briefs. His thick hard cock is inches from my mouth. As he kicks his jeans to the side, I lick him slowly and am rewarded by hot, passionate groans.

"Get on the bed, Luke."

He stretches out face down, exposing his beautiful naked backside.

I strip out of my clothes. "Not that way, honey. Face up."

"But I thought—"

"I trust you, Luke. I trust you more than anyone else in the world." I open the small nightstand drawer and retrieve the box of condoms and bottle of lubricant. "I need you inside me."

"Sweetheart, are sure?"

"Very sure."

Luke flips on his back as I place the items we need within easy reach. I can't resist but to touch him, to run my fingers through his hair, to kiss him again.

"I've been struggling for years, Luke. Yes, my parents and counselor helped keep me from completely drowning, but you were the one who carried me out of the dark water."

"Sweetheart, you did the hard work. I just put the pieces in front of you." He brushes his lips over mine. "You deserve the best in life. And I will do my best to give it to you." He runs his hands all over my body.

I do the same to him, marveling at every inch of male perfection I'm touching. I feel a hot shiver roll over me. "I want this."

"Me, too, baby."

I'm ready for him. Ready to truly become his as much as he has become mine. I rip open one of the tiny foil packages and place the condom on Luke. Then I lubricate his cock and my ass. Though we've made love with each other, I know I have to let him inside to complete our promises to one another.

Shaking, I straddle Luke, rubbing my ass against him. Feeling his cock sliding between my ass cheeks drives me insane. "I want you in my body."

"I want that more than you can imagine." Smiling, Luke strokes my cock. "I love your surprise, sweetheart."

I tweak his nipple and laugh. "I bet you do. I love you." I've never said those words to another man. Ever time I say them to him it feels so very good, so very right, so very true. It is true. I love him. He's my present. My future. My everything. I want to be his.

"I love you, Trace."

I lean forward and reach back, taking his cock in my hand. Taking a deep breath and letting it out slowly, I lean back into him. The initial piercing rocks me for a moment and I pull off of him. But instantly, my hunger for more takes over and I slide slowly down his cock, taking him inch by inch.

Our eyes are locked on one another. The caring in his brown beauties sends me to the moon. There's not an ounce of hesitation left inside me.

I ride him up and down, my need for release stronger than I've ever felt before. But I want this moment to last. This is where our connection is complete. He's mine. I'm his. We're each other's.

Careful to keep him inside me, I lean forward, delving into his mouth once again.

"God, you are so gorgeous, sweetheart," he says, latching onto my cock. He begins stroking me again.

"Yes. God, yes." I can't describe the sensations I'm feeling in my body as I go up and down him. Hot. Electric. Tingles that flow in every direction. Intense. Raising my desires to levels I've never felt before. "I want you on top of me. I need you on top of me."

I rise up on my knees and the instant he's not inside me, I go insane. I stretch out on the mattress face down, fisting the sheets. "Take me. Please. Please, Luke. I need you."

He crawls on top of me. His muscled weight feels so good. In his arms I feel safe. He slowly and carefully slides back into me. This position is different but just as intense.

"God. So good." I groan into my pillow. This rush is like no other I've ever experienced. My entire body is shaking. Every muscle is tightening. All my blood is pulsing in my veins. Every part of me is engaged in this moment with him. I need him. Having him inside me is opening me up even more. "Take me. Take me, I'm yours."

His hot groans heat the back of my neck. Every part of me is exposed, and it's okay because he is my man. He's the one who brought light into my shadowy existence.

His thrusts speed up and the pressure for release builds and builds. Every second that passes gives me new sensations, each building on top of the others that came before. I push my ass back and forth into him.

With a loud groan, Luke thrusts into me. "Fuuck."

My own release overtakes me, and I come explosively.

Feeling him kiss the back of my neck is heaven.

"I love you, Trace."

"I love you, too. Let's stay here like this for a while longer before we shower, okay?"

"Forever if you want."

Wh	en I walk into Jackson's and my apartment, I find him dusting the furniture.

I grin. "Do you ever take a break?"

"To me, this is a break. I just finished studying for my test today. Dusting is my way of relaxing."

"You're sick, but I love you. Would you please join me at the table for coffee?"

"Ah. The talk." Jackson smiles. "I knew it had to be that when you walked in. You're never up this early. Your class doesn't start for three more hours."

"I wanted to catch you before you and Ava head to class." I hand him his cup and we both sit down. "I know you and Luke already talked, but I want to make sure you are okay with me moving out. You're my best friend in the world, Jackson. I don't want to leave you high and dry."

"You're not, and you know you're my best friend too. I'm just so happy that you found Luke and he found you. You know that conversation you and I had where you told me you thought we would grow old together. That scared me, Trace."

"It did?"

LEE SWIFT

"Yes. We were getting too comfortable together. The truth is I was also imagining us growing old together. We were both settling for just friendship. I love you, buddy. Like a brother. But I don't want to spend the rest of my life with my BFF. I want what you and Luke have. I want a chance at love. I don't know if I'll find it, but seeing you two together has given me hope."

"Have you been eyeing anyone in particular?"

"Maybe."

"I thought so. Why don't you ask that sexy fireman next door out?"

Jackson grins. "How do you know I'm interested in him?"

"Oh, for crying out loud, Jackson. Everyone knows."

He shrugs. "But he's still dealing with that asshole ex of his. I don't think I have a chance with Eli until he gets that settled. And besides, there are plenty of guys out there that might be right for me."

I put my arm around his shoulders. "I agree, Jackson. Any guy would be lucky to have you in his life."

"Let's hope I find the right one." Jackson gets his iPad off the counter. "Anyway, I've put down some things we need to do for this transition." He turns the screen so we both can see. "I've already started a list of things we bought together like the vacuum cleaner and television. We can figure out how we want to split them. Are you going to take your bedroom furniture?"

"Oh my God, Jackson. Your OCD is really kicking in. I just found out I was moving in with Luke last night and you already have put a plan together. I'm not even sure when I'm moving in with him."

"Ava and I thought this weekend would be perfect."

"Are you that ready to get rid of me? It's like you're shoving me out the door."

He hugs me. "I'll never be ready, Trace. This is actually going to be hard for me, but I know it's for the best, not just for you but for me too. This is getting me out of my comfort zone, which I desperately need. And it's the start of an amazing life for you and Luke."

"Okay. Saturday it is then. We can figure out how we want to

166

divide things, what I need to take, and I what I need to leave or sell as we go."

"I wish you had a little of my OCD. You never plan anything."

"Why should I when I have you as a friend?"

He laughs.

"What about the rent? I can keep paying you until you find another roommate."

"Not necessary. Actually, I think I'm going to try living on my own for a while. I don't want another roommate, Trace. The next guy I move in to the apartment needs to be the man I spend the rest of my life with."

THE MORNING of my move to Luke's I show Jackson how organized I can be and hand him the spreadsheet I made.

His eyes widen. "I can't believe this. I guess OCD is contagious. It's all here. Everything. Items to stay. Items to take. Items to sell. And all the boxes are labeled and ready to go. Wait. Your bedroom furniture isn't on this list."

"Nope. I want you to have it. If you want to sell it now or later, the money is yours."

"You didn't have to do that, Trace, but thank you."

It doesn't take very long before all my things are moved into Unit E.

Luke places my easel by the front window downstairs. "This is where the best light is, right?"

"Yes. It's perfect there."

"Good, because I can't wait to see what you paint next." He gives me a hug.

"I don't have a clue what it's going to be, but don't you or Ava start thinking I'm crazy if either of you catch me staring at the blank canvas. It's just how my process works. Jackson got used to it, and so will you."

Ava calls to us from the kitchen. "Guys, I'm making lunch. Would one of you text Jackson to join us?"

"I'm going over there now to return my key. I'll bring him back once we do one final pass through the apartment to see if I forgot anything."

We hear little Mick through the baby monitor.

"And I'll take care of the baby," Luke says, rushing up the stairs.

I walk out the door and over to my old place.

Jackson is getting a bottle of champagne out of the fridge. "Hey, I was about to head over to your new apartment, Trace."

"That's perfect because Ava is making lunch for all of us. But I wanted to return this." I pull out my key to Unit D and hold it up for him to take.

"I want you to keep it. Who knows when I might forget something when I'm away and will need you to go inside."

"Like that's ever going to happen. I'm the one who is scatter-brained, not you. You never forget anything."

"Keep the damn key, okay. I just want you to have it."

"Okay." I can see this isn't as easy on Jackson as he thought it would be. Hell, it's not easy on me. I'm going to miss him, but I'll just be next door. "Jackson, I…well…it's just…"

"I know. For me, too. We're starting new lives. But damn it, I expect you over here every so often for coffee." He hugs me, and I hug him back.

Chapter 22

I t's only been one day since I moved into Unit E, but it already feels like home. It is home. I'm staring at the blank canvas and then it hits me what I want to paint next.

Ava finishes feeding the baby when Luke's parents call.

"Sounds great, Mom," Luke says into his phone. "We'll be there shortly to take you and Dad to dinner. Yes. Me, Ava, and Trace. Of course we're bringing the baby. Love you, too. See you soon." He puts his phone away. "Mom's anxious to see the baby."

"No wonder. This is the first time they get to see our cowboy. And I certainly can't wait to see them." Smiling, Ava stands. "Give me fifteen minutes and we'll be ready to go."

"You got it, sweetie."

She carries the baby upstairs.

Luke comes over to me. "Have you figured out what you're going to paint yet, sweetheart?"

"I have. I'm going to paint Ava and the baby, but don't tell her. I'd like to surprise her with it later."

"My lips are sealed." He kisses me.

"Should I change?" I look down at my clothes. "I want to make a good first impression with your parents."

"You look great in those jeans, sweetheart. Dad always wears jeans, too. Don't worry, Mom and Dad are going to love you."

"I hope so. I bet most of their attention is going to be on our little Mick more than me anyway."

"Probably. This is their first grandchild."

Ava comes down with the baby and we leave for the hotel where Luke's parents are staying. When we arrive, we find them waiting for us in the lobby. Luke has his dad's eyes and his mom's smile. His dad has on a cowboy hat and jeans, just like Luke said. His mom is wearing slacks and a colorful top. They're a very attractive couple. I can see where Luke gets his good looks.

Mr. and Mrs. Wagner head right for the baby, which is no surprise to us.

His mom takes little Mick from Ava. "Look at you. Daryl, this is Mick's son, our grandson. Can you believe it?"

"Hey, handsome. Looking good, just like your dad and old grandpa."

I can see tears welling up in their eyes. The pain of losing their son clearly still lingers.

Mr. Wagner hugs Ava. "How are you doing, sweetie?"

"I'm very busy with going to school and taking care of the baby. But thanks to Luke's and Trace's help, I'm doing great."

"Hey son." He hugs Luke and then turns to me. "And you must be Trace, the guy my boy can't stop talking about."

"Hello, sir. Nice to meet you." I extend my hand.

"Oh, that won't do." He smiles. "I'm small town. We hug." He pulls me in for a warm welcome.

Mrs. Wagner won't let go of the baby, but gives me a kiss on the cheek. "Man, you're a good-looking guy. No wonder you caught my son's eye."

"Thank you, Mrs. Wagner, and you're a very beautiful lady."

"Please call me Mom, Trace. You're part of the family now."

"I agree, Kay," Mr. Wagner says. "And call me Dad."

"I'd be happy to."

Mom winks at Luke and me. "I expect to hear wedding bells any day now, right?"

Luke shakes his head. "Mom, you sure don't beat around the bush do you?"

"No, and I don't intend to start now." She smiles. "Have you made plans yet?"

"Kay, leave these boys alone," Mr. Wagner says. "They'll tell us when they pick a date."

I grin, seeing Luke start to squirm. "We haven't talked about that yet. We only moved in together yesterday."

"Oh. I see. Living in sin?" Her laugh is music to my ears. "We better take care of that."

"Guys, take it from me," Ava says. "When Mom wants something, there's no stopping her until she gets it."

"Well, who knows what might happen while they're here." Luke puts his arm around me. "But right now the big decision is where we are going to eat. What are you in the mood for?"

"I could really go for a thick, juicy steak," Dad answers.

"I know just the place," I tell him. "Dunn and Stan's Steak House on Lovers Avenue."

"Let's go. I'm starving." Dad holds out his keys. "Who's driving? I'm not familiar with Dallas."

"Trace, do you mind driving Dad," Mom says. "I'm going with Luke and Ava because I want to be with the baby."

"I don't mind at all. It would be my pleasure."

"Okay, Grandma," Dad says. "Just as long as I get to be with him on the drive back."

She grins. "Maybe. I'm not sure I can let this sweet bundle out of my sight."

"This is how it's going down, Kay." He puts his arm around her and looks straight into her eyes. "I'm going to hold my grandson whether you like it or not."

I love how Luke's parents tease each other. It's clear they are very much in love.

"I'll have to follow you, Trace." Luke kisses me lightly on the cheek. "I don't know where this steak house is either."

"Not a problem. It's not far from here."

We walk out of the hotel lobby. As Luke, Ava, his mom, and the baby get into the truck, Dad takes me to his car, a silver Cadillac.

"Nice ride, Dad."

"I'm glad you like it."

We hop in and take off.

On the way to the restaurant, he says, "Trace, I'm so glad you and Luke are together. I haven't seen him this happy since we lost Mick. Actually, I've never seen him this happy before. I like what you bring out in him."

"I'm happy, too. I'm crazy about your son. He helped me with some issues I had that I'd like to share with you sometime. He's a wonderful man."

"That makes two of you. So, I'm thinking a spring wedding would make my wife happy, do you agree?"

I laugh. "So she's not the only one we need to be worried about."

"That's for sure. I think I can speak for Kay, Trace. We knew a lot about you before we met, but now, after seeing you in person, it's plain as day. You're the one for our Luke. And you're bringing light into our lives as well. Seeing Mick's son in Kay's arms and you standing next to Luke has brought joy into this old man's heart." He wipes the tears from his eyes.

His words are so moving to me as I drive down the road.

"Son, we'll never stop missing Mick, but now I realize that this family has a bright future ahead with you and little Mick in it. So welcome to the family."

I feel tears welling up in my eyes.

"Here, Son. Take this." He hands me his handkerchief. "You're driving."

Once we get to the restaurant, Dad finally holds the baby. Mom asks me to sit next to her.

Luke leans over and whispers, "What do you think of my parents?"

"I'm crazy about them almost as much as I'm crazy about their son."

THE NEXT MORNING, I make a big breakfast for Jackson, Ava, Luke, and his parents. Sausage, eggs, hash browns, biscuits and gravy, and pancakes for those of us with a sweet tooth.

"Who taught you how to cook, young man?" Dad asks me, taking another biscuit.

"My mother and father are both incredible cooks. I learned everything from them, but breakfast has always been my specialty."

"Well, I must say this is absolutely delicious."

Mom holds the baby. "I agree. Daryl and I would love to meet your parents some time, Trace."

"Actually, they're going to be back home tomorrow. Maybe we can set up a barbeque in the courtyard for after class."

Luke shakes his head. "No barbeque tomorrow, sweetheart, though your parents are coming over."

"What? What are you talking about?"

Jackson laughs. "I thought you were going to keep it secret, Luke."

"He never can," Ava says with a smile. "Luke is only able to keep quiet for about two days. After that, he can't help but blab."

"That's not true, sweetie. I'm telling Trace because he's bound to find out anyway. They're putting up the tents today in the courtyard."

"I'm totally confused. What tents?"

"The ones Oliver borrowed from the university."

"That doesn't tell me anything. Why in the world are there going to be tents in the courtyard? What is this secret? Come on, guys. Fill me in. Don't leave me in the dark. And how do you know my parents are coming over tomorrow, Luke?"

"Because I talked to them."

"Trace, I gave your parents' number to Luke," Jackson says. "He had something he wanted to say to them."

Luke hugs me. "You remember when I said I had an idea about your paintings the other day? Tomorrow evening after you get back from class, Mockingbird Place's residences are hosting an art show of your paintings in the courtyard."

"Are you serious?"

"Yes, sweetheart. Very serious."

I wrap my arms around him. "You're the most wonderful man in the world. I'm so lucky. I love you."

"I love you, too."

We kiss.

Mom asks the baby, "Don't you think this is the perfect time for one of your uncles to get down on their knee, my sweet angel?" She turns to Luke and me. "He says yes."

"Kay." Dad shakes his head.

"Don't shoot the messenger, honey. Just relaying what little Mick wants." She grins.

We all laugh.

And then it's like lightning strikes me. I love Luke. He loves me. We want to spend the rest of our lives with each other. Why not get down on my knee and ask him? So I do, and so does he—at the exact same time.

At first I hear a few chuckles from Ava and his parents, and then it's like Luke and I are the only two people in the world.

"Trace, this isn't how I planned to ask you." He takes my hands and gazes at me with those gorgeous eyes of his. "I had this elabo-rate idea that included a carriage ride and a candlelight dinner under the stars."

"That's funny because I imagined taking you out on a sailboat at White Rock Lake, opening a bottle of wine, and reciting poetry to you." I smile. "Either one sounds wonderful, but it doesn't matter, Luke. We're here now on our knees facing each other."

"We are. I love you so much. You astonish me, sweetheart. Besides being the most handsome man I've ever seen, you also have the biggest heart I've ever known. You care deeply for your family and friends. With you I'm just better—a better person, a better man, a better everything. You mean the world to me. You are my world. Please, marry me."

Running over with joy, I squeeze his hand. "Luke, I was lost before you came into my life, going through the motions, pasting a smile on my face every day, trying to get by and trying to forget. You saw things in me that no one ever saw, things even I was blind to. I thought I was lesser than everyone else—that my past and present could only end up in a gray and lonely future. But then you moved into Unit E with Ava and turned my world upside down and sideways. You shined a light into me and I will never be the same. I want you. I need you. I want to spend the rest of my life in your arms. Yes, I will marry you. Will you marry me, you sexy beast?"

"Of course I will marry you, baby."

We kiss.

The clapping pulls my attention back to the fact that we are not alone. Jackson, Ava, Dad, and Mom, who is still holding the baby, surround us.

"I've got another bottle of champagne at my place," Jackson says, heading for the door. "This definitely requires a toast."

"I'll get the glasses." Ava opens the cabinet.

"Pictures, Daryl," Mom says. "We need pictures."

"On it, sweetheart." He pulls out his phone and begins snapping photos of Luke and me.

"Dad, would you mind sending one of those pictures to me?" I ask him. "I'm anxious to talk to my parents and let them know Luke and I are engaged. I know they would want a picture."

"Of course, but let's give them the perfect one. Okay, guys. Get back down on your knees like you were a moment ago."

I grin and look at Luke. "We're in trouble now, aren't we?"

He kisses me. "You bet we are."

As we pose for Dad, I realize I've never been happier than I am right now.

Chapter 23

L *uke — the day of the art show.*

JACKSON OPENS THE LAST BOX. He's been helping me so much with the art show.

"What about this one, Luke?" Jackson holds up the painting. It's a beach scene with a boy and his dog.

"I think that goes in the tent with all the landscapes, but ask my mom or Martha to be sure."

He nods and walks out of the apartment with the painting.

It took some convincing, but Trace finally agreed we could sell his works. He wasn't sure what price to ask for any of them, so I called one of his professors who helped us with the prices.

Trace was shocked at how much Professor Adams suggested but went along with it. "If they don't sell, so be it. I'll just put them back in storage or give them away to friends and family."

Knowing Trace's parents will be arriving any moment, I quickly straighten the living room.

Ava is upstairs with the baby and Trace is getting dressed. Everybody else is pitching in to make sure this show is perfect for Trace. Even my mom and dad. They're helping S & M decide which paintings go in what tent. Eli, Jaris, and Tony are manning the beverages. Harvey is finishing up the lighting so that every one of Trace's pieces are beautifully lit. The rest of our neighbors are doing whatever else needs to be done.

Trace comes down the stairs holding two shirts on hangers.

"Luke, which one should I wear tonight?" He seems anxious. "Are khakis okay or should I put on a pair of slacks? And what about these shirts? Which one do you like? I also need your opinion on shoes? What time is it?"

"Slow down, sweetheart, and breathe." I put my arm around him and kiss his cheek. "Let's take one question at a time. It's only 5:00. So you have two and a half hours to decide, but I personally think that since this is an outside event, the khakis and the blue shirt would be perfect. And they would go great with your brown loafers."

The doorbell rings.

"It's open," I yell. "Come on in."

I look over my shoulder and see an attractive couple walk in.

Trace's eyes light up. "Mom, Dad, glad you're here." He hands me the shirts, walks over to them, and gives them a big hug. "I missed you. How was your trip?"

"It was great, but just look at you." His mother steps back. "I haven't seen you this happy in a long time." Then she looks at me. "And this is the guy responsible for putting the smile on your face. Hello, Luke." She gives me a hug. "My goodness, you are good-looking, aren't you?"

"That's funny, Mom. His mother said the same thing about me."

She smiles. "Then she must be a very intelligent woman. I can't wait to meet her."

I like her wit and attitude. "Mom is definitely going to love you. Could I get you something to drink?"

Trace's dad shakes my hand. "No thanks. We're here to help

with setting up your fiancé's art show, young man. I'm ready to roll up my sleeves and get to work."

As if on cue, my mom and dad walk into the apartment.

"Oh my goodness," Trace's mother says. "You must be Daryl and Kay, Luke's parents."

My mom nods. "And you must be Rich and Donna, Trace's parents."

Everyone hugs each other.

Dad pats Rich on the back. "It's so good to meet you on such an important occasion."

"Are you talking about the engagement or the art show?" Rich sits down.

"Both. I'm so happy for these boys. They've helped each other so much."

Mom squeezes Donna's hand. "You and I have so much planning to do for their wedding."

"You're right about that." Donna places her tote on the sofa and pulls out her phone. "Kay, we need to exchange numbers."

"Yes, we do." Mom gets out her phone. After they share their numbers with each other, Mom says, "And now we need to make sure that sweet son of yours has the best art show ever. Daryl and I invited everyone we know who lives in Dallas to come. There are also some friends driving in from home to be here today."

"Where's home?" Rich asks.

Dad takes a seat next to him. "San Angelo."

"Where are you and Kay staying while you're in town?"

"At a hotel nearby."

Rich turns to Donna. "That won't do, will it, sweetheart?"

"No, it won't. Family is not put up in hotels. The boys' place is too small, but Rich and I have plenty of room in our house. It's only ten minutes away."

As our parents make plans to spend more time together, Trace whispers to me, "It's like they've known each other their entire lives."

"Yes, it is. Your parents are great."

"So are yours," Trace says. "Their personalities are very much alike."

Ava comes down the stairs with the baby. "Hi."

"Hey, sweetheart." My mom grabs Donna's hand. "Let me introduce you to my sweet daughter-in-law and my first grandbaby."

Our four parents surround her and little Mick, cooing and talking gibberish with big smiles.

"It looks like those four have never seen a baby before." Trace laughs.

He seems more relaxed, which pleases me.

"Would you like to hold him?" Ava asks Donna.

"I would love too. Trace, would you get my tote bag off the chair? I have something for the baby."

"That's so sweet of you, Donna."

Carrying the tote, Trace steps next to his mom.

"Would you mind giving the present to Ava?" Donna kisses the baby's forehead.

Trace lifts out the box and hands it to Ava.

She unwraps the gift and holds up a sweet blue blanket with images of teddy bears and rocking horses. "I love it. Thank you, Donna. Thank you, Rich."

The baby starts fussing.

"I knew it was time to feed him, but I wanted to say hello first," Ava says. "I guess I better take him back upstairs."

"I hate to let him go, but I guess I must. At least for now." Donna hands him back to her.

After Ava takes the baby into her room, Rich stands. "Donna and I have never seen my son's paintings before, and I'd like to take a look at them before the crowd arrives."

Dad also stands. "Rich, Trace is so talented." He looks at Mom. "Kay, why don't you and I give Donna and Rich the tour of the tents?"

"A perfect idea. That will give Luke and Trace some time alone before the show starts."

The four of them walk out together.

"I think they bonded on the spot, Trace."

"Yes, they did." He looks at the time on his phone. "I know you said the khakis and blue shirt, but I'd like to try them on before I decide. Would you help me make a decision?"

"You know I will." I would do anything for him. Anything.

Most of the time Trace isn't so picky about his clothes, but since this day is about him and his art, he wants to make sure he looks perfect. After going through several outfits, Trace finally agrees with me and settles on the one I suggested earlier.

I take a long look at him. "You look perfect, sweetheart. I know this is going to be a great success. I love you." I can't resist and lean in and give him a romantic kiss.

"I love you, too, you sexy beast."

Just before seven, I lead him out of the apartment and into the courtyard.

People are already arriving. We see Alvin and the other guys walking into one of the tents. Some of Trace's professors, including Professor Adams, who helped us with the pricing, are talking with S & M.

He kisses me. "Thank you for doing this. I love you, honey."

"I love you, too."

Jaris walks over to us. "Luke, I need to steal him from you for a moment. I want to introduce Trace to the reporter from the *Dallas Morning News*."

"Steal away," I say.

Trace's eyes widen. "Reporter? Here?"

"Yes here, baby. For you. Go do your magic."

Jaris leads him to a woman standing in the tent with the portraits.

After I asked everyone in the complex if they knew anyone in the media they could invite to Trace's art show, Jaris told us he did and would be happy to invite the reporter. Being from a wealthy local family, Jaris is very well connected in Dallas. I can't help but wonder why he chooses to live at Mockingbird Place. It's obvious he could afford just about any place in town—a chic new condo in Uptown or a high-rise apartment on Turtle Creek.

I'm thrilled to see Trace smile as he talks to the reporter. I watch as more and more people arrive for the show. This is going even better than I dreamed.

A couple hours later, the show is starting to wind down.

Over half of Trace's paintings sold. He's made a lot of money. His professor is certain Trace is going to become a very well-known artist in Dallas and says that at the next showing, Trace should definitely raise his prices.

I glance over at Trace. He's talking with Alvin and the other guys who were at the school with us. Alvin bought the painting of the lion chasing the gazelle. Each of the other guys also bought paintings.

"You must be very pleased with how the show turned out," Harvey says, moving next to me.

"Very pleased. Trace is happy, which makes me happy."

"I'm glad for you both. Everyone is so excited about your wedding."

"You've been talking to our moms, right?"

"Yes, I have. We all have." Harvey glances at the memorial tree for Malcolm.

I put my arm around him. "I'm so glad Trace gave you the portrait of Malcolm."

"I tried to pay him for it, but Trace said absolutely not. Told me it was a gift. Said he didn't want anyone else to have it." Harvey wipes the tears from his eyes. "You and Trace deserve happiness. I wish you a long and wonderful life together."

As I watch Harvey walk away, Trace comes up beside me with a big smile on his face. "Honey, can you believe I'm going to be in the *Dallas Morning News*?"

"That's fantastic, sweetheart."

He wraps his arms around me. "There's something more fantastic than that, Luke. We made a bundle. Would you like to take a honeymoon around the world or would you rather buy our own house?"

I give him a kiss. "Let's get married first, sweetheart."

Chapter 24

*J*ackson McAllen—*a month later.*

AFTER SPENDING several hours at the university's library, I pull into my parking space, anxious to get into my apartment and warm bed. It's been a very long and cold winter day. The car is registering the outside temperature at ten degrees below freezing. It gives me a chill just looking at it. Yawning, I open my car door and immediately smell smoke.

I look around and see where it's coming from. Shit. It's Eli's apartment.

God, I hope he's at the fire station working and not inside.

I call 9-1-1.

The dispatcher answers, "9-1-1. What's your emergency?"

"I'm reporting a fire at Mockingbird Place." I give her the address. "Unit C. I'm going to run to the door and make sure no one is inside."

"Sir, for your safety you need to wait until the fire department gets there," she says in a stern voice.

As I'm running, I tell her, "No way am I waiting." At Eli's door, I try to turn the knob. It's locked. I pound as hard as I can. "Eli! Eli! Are you in there?"

My neighbors come out of their apartments. More smoke billows out the front window. I see that it's broken. This could be arson. That realization multiplies my worry. Where the hell are you, Eli?

"I know I'm not supposed to hang up on you, ma'am, but I have to call my friend to make sure he's okay." Not waiting for her to respond, I click off of 9-1-1 and call Eli's phone.

Sirens begin to wail in the distance.

Fuck. No answer.

About the Author

Lee Swift, who writes under several pen names including Kris Cook, creates novels, short stories, screenplays and more.

With an unquenchable thirst to experience all his life journey has to offer, Lee and hubby love travel but still call Dallas, Texas home.

Join [HERE] to get updates on Lee.

Also by Lee Swift

Novels

Morvicti Blood *(Supernatural Thriller)*

Cupid's Arrow *(Gay Fantasy Romance)*

Three to Play *(Menage MMF Romance)*

(All series listed in best reading order)

Mockingbird Place

(Gay Romance Series)

The Marine in Unit A

The Cowboy in Unit E

The Fireman in Unit C

The Doctor in Unit H

The Fighter in Unit J

Holiday Beaus (Novella)

The Musician in Unit G

The Cop in Unit B

Wolf Pack

(Menage MFM Romance Trilogy)

Secret Cravings

Primal Desires

Delicious Hunger

Eternal Trio Series

(Gay Menage Fantasy Romance)

Levi's Rogues

Perfection

Writing with Lana Lynn
(Thrillers)

Lexi's Protector *(Men Without A Cause)*

Liz's Guardian *(Men Without A Cause)*

Secret Diary Series as Kris Cook
(Erotic Straight BDSM Trilogy)

Mia's Spanking Diary

Misty's Bondage Diary

Lea's Ménage Diary

www.ingramcontent.com/pod-product-compliance
Lightning Source LLC
Chambersburg PA
CBHW020959180626
46814CB00003B/1163